ZERO DEGREE

by CHARU NIVEDITA

translated from the Tamil by
PRITHAM K. CHAKRAVARTHY
and
RAKESH KHANNA

PUBLICATIONS
PRIVATE LIMITED
Chennai

English translation first published in India in 2008 by
Blaft Publications Pvt. Ltd.

First printing May 2008
Second printing January 2009

ISBN 978 81 906056 1 8

Blaft Publications Pvt. Ltd.
#27 Lingam Complex
Dhandeeswaram Main Road
Velachery
Chennai 600042
email: blaft@blaft.com

Printed in India at
Sudarshan Graphics, Chennai

Translators' Note

We would like to let *Zero Degree* speak for itself, after taking just a moment to disavow our personal support for any political agenda that this book or its characters may have, and also to point out two idiosyncratic difficulties the book posed for the translator.

First, in keeping with the numerological theme of *Zero Degree*, the only numbers expressed in either words or symbols are numerologically equivalent to nine (with the exception of two chapters). This Oulipian ban includes the very common Tamil word ஒரு, *one*, used very much like the English *one* ("one day", "one of them", etc.) The way Charu Nivedita works around this constraint in Tamil is a notable feature of the original text. However, Tamil has some better substitutes for this word than English does. For instance, there are two pronouns each for *he* and *she:* அவன்/அவள் (roughly "that man"/"that woman") and இவன்/இவள் ("this man"/"this woman"). The lack of single-word English equivalents sometimes results in less graceful constructions than Tamil makes possible. We have done our best to make these sentences easily readable without using the forbidden numbers.

Secondly, many sections of the book are written entirely without punctuation, or using only periods. This reminds the Tamil reader of an ancient style of writing, before Western punctuation marks were adopted into the script. However, in English, omitting punctuation, besides being confusing, would fail to give this effect. Therefore, we have inserted punctuation marks in many chapters, except where it seemed important to the meaning of the text to leave them out.

Zero Degree was first published in Chennai in 1998. It is the author's second novel, and features many of the same characters that appeared in his first, *Existentialism and Fancy Banyan*. It did well enough for a second and third edition, and was also translated into Malayalam by Balasubramaniam and P. M. Girish. In Kerala, the book generated a great deal of...

[*The remainder of the translators' note was destroyed by a computer virus.*]

Pritham K. Chakravarthy

Rakesh Khanna

The English version of this book is dedicated
to the memory of Kathy Acker

बुद्धिर्ज्ञानमसम्मोहः क्षमा सत्यं दमः शमः ।
सुखं दुःखं भवोऽभावो भयं चाभयमेव च ॥४॥
अहिंसा समता तुष्टिस्तपो दानं यशोऽयशः ।
भवन्ति ावा भूतानां मत्त एव पृथग्विधाः ॥५॥

*Reason, wisdom, lucid thinking, tolerance, truth,
temperance in thought and body, pleasure, pain,
destruction, fear, courage, non-violence, equality,
contentment, renunciation, charity, praise, disdain—all
human qualities begin with Me.*

—Bhagavad Gita, 10:4-5

0°

PRAYER

My Dear Genny,

I stand outside the real world at this moment, and I think of how very long it has been since I spoke to you.

I recall the words you said, just before we separated for the last time: "Appa, you'll come to see me, won't you?"

We did not know that would be our last meeting.

My dear daughter, what could I ever give you that would be worthy of those tears, the tears that hung from your eyes like drops of dew...?

That first tear drop made me realize that there was still warmth left in my dry life.

I have compiled 1800 pages of conversations with my women friends and lady readers, and of my own history. Most of these pages were discarded, but what remains, I send to you now. I have no way of knowing if these words will make it past the snow-capped mountains to reach you.

Having thus burdened your tender heart with the ancestral brutality of man, I trek alone through the snowy wasteland, not knowing if it is day or night.

It has been ages since I have uttered or heard human speech. I will not say that silence is protecting me. I believe that the strain of music at the very bottom of that silence is what still keeps me alive.

Or perhaps...

my heart is still beating only because of you.

You created this misty desert.

You *are* Creation.

I hope that the vacuum of this dialogue I had with creation will come alive in the reading.

It is only your tender touch that can revive my life, a life that is slowly slipping away...

0°

Chapter 1

My Dear Lady Reader, as you begin to read this text, *0°*, you may be...

- lying on your tummy fantasizing about your wedding.

- writing a poem or a letter.

- puzzling in front of the typewriter over the impenetrable notes your boss has dictated.

- traveling by bus, train, or car.

- quarrelling with your husband over the telephone.

- walking across hot wet tar, wearing gunny sacks as socks on your feet, to fill the potholes in the road with rubble.

- sitting at the edge of a pond in which the water is warm on top but cool lower down, with your skirt tucked around your knees, flapping your feet in the water.

- working at a granite quarry.

- yawning in a biology lecture.

- lying in a deep coma in the hospital.

- picking at your wounds in a lunatic asylum corridor.

- swallowing sleeping pills.

- fretting, alone, after a divorce, refusing to sacrifice any more of your life for a man.

- sitting amidst ninety sewing machines, pedaling, and sighing when your thighs rub hard against each other.

- skipping rope to give yourself an abortion.

- dropping a stone on the head of your son who dared to spy on you and your lover.

- branding your daughter's thighs with a red-hot iron rod.

- plotting your dishonest husband's murder.

- demonstrating the dance steps choreographed by the dance master to the irritated heroine, for the ninth time, at an outdoor location, in the hot sun.

- wondering whether the whiskey breath of the hero kissing you is left over from last night or is from this morning's shot.

- at your office desk, chewing your lips because of menstrual cramps.

- milking a cow.

- trekking with a group.

- copulating with your best friend.

- laying your baby on a sheet at the street corner and begging.

- drinking beer with your boyfriend.

- manicuring your nails.

- o   removing hair from your armpits with **Anne French***.

- o   dreaming about having sex with your brother, or God.

- o   planning on offering only your clenched thighs, instead of your hole, to the ninth customer of the day.

- o   burning a literary journal.

- o   berating the eunuch who refuses to give you your cut of the money, using forbidden swear words relating to the genitals.

- o   smoking ganja.

- o   rolling a beedi.

- o   filling matchboxes with matchsticks.

- o   breastfeeding your baby.

- o   knocking on a stranger's door to sell a new soap product.

- o   discussing Helen Cioux with your friend.

- o   rehearsing for the part of Claire in *Maids*.

- o   reading the paragraph on **CUNT** in *Madwoman's Underclothes*.

- o   blacking out the breasts visible on the dirty poster.

- o   kneading cow dung with your feet to make dung cakes.

- o   listening to Kenny G on your walkman.

- o   carefully carving out the yolk from your fried egg.

---

* Translator's Note: Throughout the text, boldface type is used to indicate English printed in Roman letters in the original.

- screaming because your husband's mother is holding you down while your husband douses you in kerosene and throws a lit match onto you.

- swallowing oleander seeds because you failed in your exams.

- suddenly happening upon your mother fucking a stranger in the living room.

- eloping with your lover.

- cowering in a corner as your customer disrobes in front of you.

- thinking about space, while the hero spins a top on your navel and the camera records a tight close-up.

- training to be a terrorist.

- groaning because a prick as large as a wild banana is being shoved down your throat for a porno film shoot.

- disgusted with the hero who is groping at the exposed part of your breast, just above your skimpy blouse.

- chanting "Sriramajayam."

- buying tickets on the black market for your favorite film.

- losing consciousness because nine policemen have stripped you in front of your husband and are now raping you continuously.

- screaming in labor pain.

- sticking a vibrator up your pussy.

- clenching your butt cheeks around the prick being rubbed in your crack on a crowded bus.

0°

CHAPTER 2

THE "I" THAT APPEARS at the beginning of this novel refers to me, Charu Nivedita, the author. But there are actually several other "I"s responsible for the book. First of all, there is Surya, who wanted to write a novelization of the life of Muniyandi, and dedicate it to his daughter, Genesis; he made pages and pages of notes, and pasted in lots of clippings from the daily newspapers. Then there is Muniyandi himself, who later went through Surya's notes and made all sorts of corrections and revisions. But this material alone could never have been organized into a complete novel. In the tangled mess, it is often confusing who the "I" refers to—sometimes it is Muniyandi, other times it is Surya, other times it is simply lost in a fog.

To confuse things further, there is even a third "I": Misra—the same Misra who, in each of the 999 copies of *Existentialism and Fancy Banyan*, commits suicide on page 144. A few days before he actually went in for suicide, he, too, was thinking of writing a book, and had started collecting material for it. Many parts of this novel are taken from his Hindi notes, and so it is possible to think of it as a novel translated from Hindi. I was not, however, able to bring the exact essence of the Hindi into Tamil—e.g., lines like *mayi avaa behen thi land maa thi land maa thi phutthi* were very difficult. Please, dear Lady Reader, do forgive me for that.

My guru in translation was a fellow named Kottikuppan. When I was in primary school, we used to walk from our village to the school in groups of four or five, and Kottikuppan would come along as our escort. The path to the school from our village was long, and passed through the cremation ground. We were very scared of the cremation ground; that was where the dead roamed as ghosts. But Kottikuppan was brave. He feared nothing.

Do not assume, just because I speak of him so familiarly, that Kottikuppan was a young boy. Sami Sir guessed that he might be around thirty-six. Sami Sir had settled in our village after he retired from the military, and Kottikuppan, too, had arrived there a long time ago. My mother used to say that even though he looked as though he was in the ninth standard, he was really as old as a donkey.

Dey Kottikuppan, what's your age.

Age means vayasu, page means pakkam, cage means koondu, tej means light, mez means table, roz means anger, wage means income.

Which place are you from.

Place means edam, space also means edam, face means mokam, race means ottam, case means case.

Well means kenaru, wall means suvaru, wool means kambli, pull means izhu, full means fullu.

Talk means pechu, walk means nadai, chalk means chalkpiece, cock means kunju, lock means poottu, rock means malai.

He would talk like this until we had crossed the cremation ground. The way he talked, it was almost as if he had come to our village to enlighten the illiterate villagers. Give him work, and he would never refuse; he fed the cows and hens, herded the goats, dried dung cakes, cut wood, carried crying babies on his shoulder and pointed at the moon, plucked coconuts from the trees. But when he spoke it was nothing but *randi nondi sondi pandi mandi kundi sandi kindi kendi...* just that. It never went beyond that.

As I write this it strikes me that Kottikuppan was perhaps the world's last great translator. It is on the basis of what he taught me that I managed to translate Misra's Hindi and Muniyandi's butler English and link them to Surya's Tamil notes. I took enormous license in editing out most of those notes; I even contributed some of my own. I have taken all those "I"s and added my own "I" to them. My dear Lady Reader, you may add your own to them as well. Or...

0°

CHAPTER 3

What follows is a collection of notes gathered for a 999-page historical novel that is yet to be written:

Presently the Kasarmanians are massacring the Karmenians in the regions of Bucharek and Nazorno in Kasarmania. The Karmenians are retaliating by killing Kasarmanians. This feud, which owes its origins to religious differences, has been going on for two thousand seven hundred years. The total Karmenian population today is thirty-six lakhs, many of whom form a minority population in the north Caucasus. Of these, around eighteen lakhs have migrated to Greece, Syria, France and America. As far back as 900 B.C., the area was home to a well-organized state. Later, however, the Romans and Parthians began warring with each other for control of Karmenia, and a massive genocide ensued. In 333 A.D., the Parthian Empire was destroyed, and the Sassanid Empire began to rise. The Karmenians converted to Christianity very early, even during the time of Christ. The Arabs intruded into the Caucasus in 702 A.D. and ushered in an era of prolonged war and much bloodshed. Karmenia was conquered by the Tsar of Russia in 1800. In 1818, a long contest began between the Tsar and Iran; the east of Karmenia remained with Russia, but large portions of the land were annexed by Turkey and Iran. In 1917 the Turkish parts of Karmenia disappeared from the face of the Earth. Of the 27 lakhs of Karmenians living there, 18 lakhs were butchered. The

9 lakh survivors escaped to Mesopotamia where a further 5.4 lakhs were massacred; of the survivors, 1.8 lakhs fled to Russia, and 1.8 lakhs to Europe. Then followed an internal struggle, in which the Kasarmanians killed some 54 lakh Karmenians. Many Kasarmanians were killed in retaliation, and so a long ethnic struggle proceeded, with much killing on both sides. Human bodies were axed, tongues hewn, arms amputated, stomachs gouged out, breasts torn apart, yonis speared with red-hot iron rods. Countless bodies were burned. Masses of half-cooked corpses lay around in piles. The grandson spake thusly: "When a banyan tree falls, of course the Earth will quake." The words sprouted wings and flew off: *tree earth quakes falls tree falls quakes earth tree earth falls quakes earth tree quakes falls quakes earth falls tree quakes tree falls earth.* The religious leader cautioned women against wearing silk saris and footwear, saying that the making of such articles necessitates the torture of animals, which is, of course, a sin.

—in which thirty-six bodies of young men were found, riddled with bullet wounds or half-burned. The police reported that the Death Squad was responsible for this massacre—forty-five kilometers from there, twenty-seven bodies were removed from a stack of burning car tyres. The villagers said that these murders had occurred during curfew. Eighteen badly burned bodies were found in the fields. During his Switzerland tour, at a press meet at the airport, the Foreign Minister declared however that the military had absolutely no connection with any Death Squad involved in the massacre of young

How about that kabadi sequence that Ravi Ragul and Vinodhini play in *Aatha Un Koyilile*? When I saw that, I wanted to join the game! This is a perfect example of what a good film scene should be like; it should make us want to identify with it. Ammu is the pet of Kalasri, who was featured in *En Pottukku Sondhakaaran* (ah! what a film), *Ponnuketha Mannu*, *Ponnuketha Purushan*, and *En Purushan Thaan Enakku Mattum Thaan*. This is what Kalasri says about her Ammu:

I hate pigs. My friend Priyasri rears pedigreed pigs, and that's why I never go to her house. Recently, my

men. He also promised that when he returned to the homeland after twenty-seven days, he would order the army to take action against those responsible for these strange murders. I spoke to the young girl picking up shattered glass on the street near the gutter. She was from Chennai. She spoke Hindi fluently. She could find no employment in Chennai. She was now living with her uncle in Patpar Ganj. She earned eighteen paisa per kilo of broken glass shards and ninety paisa per kilo of scraps of tin. [Lady Reader, remember that Misra is writing this in the 1980s.] Those mountains resembled bald heads. Anjum says there are eighteen thousand bonded laborers. Their daily wage is a mere Rs. 1.80. What the bosses say goes. The youngsters among the bonded laborers were identified as guerilla rebels by the police and around 2700 of them were shot down. Swamis clad in loincloths roam these hills, considering them to be the hills of Shiva. I came to Karim Nagar district with Anjum. If ninety beedi leaves are rolled into a bundle the wage is ninety paisa. *Arrey baapre!* The Patwaris grab poromboke land away from the villagers. When the villagers protest,

mother brought me a piglet and told me, 'Kala, keep her.' Since then she has been my house pet. When she was still very young, she refused to eat anything solid, and wanted only a liquid diet. So I would carry her in my arms and feed her milk from a bottle. She would feed well. What I loved most of all was her beautiful (anus) mouth. Even though her entire body was black, the (anus) mouth would sparkle like a pink cherry. Only when Ammu was in a bad mood would she eat carrots and cabbage. When you carry other animals, you have to support their whole body. But Ammu would let you carry her by her ears. Ammu was very special. She used to leap into my arms. When I ate, she would stand and sniff at me behind my chair. Every Friday, I would wash her down with a wet rag. But I forgot to tell you this: in front of my bungalow was this slum, which was the source of my problem. Because the people who live in the slums have no understanding of sanitation, they shit and piss in the streets. Listen to this, no... On that day Ammu slipped out without my knowledge and ate some of the shit. I fired the careless watchman that very same day. I even attempted to commit suicide by swallowing sleeping pills. I was saved, the police are called, false charges are filed, and the village women are raped. Of course, if I continue to write like this you will call it newspaper reportage. But you celebrate an American who does the same as a writer of New Journalism. What can I do? A daily wager was gunned down. Nine shots were heard. The body had nine gunshot wounds. The police reported that when he grabbed a rifle away from a policeman and tried to shoot them, the other police had to gun him down. But in reality he was dragged out of his house and shot down in full view of his neighbors on the street, in broad daylight. If I claim that this is true they will call me a naxalite and eliminate me. But when a feudal lord was shot in Huzarabad, 270 were arrested, of whom 63 were indicted.

though, as the pills turned out to be vitamin pills. If they hadn't been, you would not be able to speak to your favorite star Kalasri today.

The following is the response of Neelasri, Kalasri's co-actress, to her interview:

Kalasri's claims about Ammu's diet are pure fabrication. I know for a fact that Ammu's favorite food is shit. That's why Kalasri does not have a flush-out latrine in her house. Ammu is the reason that Kalasri's manually-cleared latrine is cleaner than our Western toilet. I think she has admitted to this in her interview without realizing it. Just read what she has said. 'When I ate, she would stand and sniff at me behind my chair.'

When asked what Kalasri could have meant by "sniff at me behind," Neelasri's eyes burned with indignation. This is Kalasri's rejoinder to Neelasri: *She's just jealous of my success, and has therefore spread poisonous gossip about me and my Ammu. What good are people who wag their tongues so irresponsibly about helpless beings?* she demanded, and the tears in her eyes were real, not produced with the help of glycerin.

$0°$

REFLECTION

THERE HAS BEEN A MISTAKE, Genesis. In my enthusiasm to put the novel together, the chapters have become shuffled. Now that I think about it, I might have had some ulterior motive. Perhaps my hatred for Muniyandi and my love for Misra are responsible; perhaps I've subconsciously moved Misra ahead and shoved Muniyandi to the background. What should have come later came in the beginning, and pushed what should have been the beginning into the future. How do I escape from this confusion of time? Costa Rica's María Fernández de Tinoco says the past is getting erased; written words are rubbed out again and again and reduced to nothingness. Like ink on a blotting paper, the past dissipates from the pages of my memory. I return to the nothingness with no recollections. The past has pushed me aside and gone into hiding.

Still, I think a moment may come when I will be able to capture the past. That moment may arrive at any time, Genny—perhaps even as you are reading this sentence. And at that instant only you and this text will remain; I, who wrote it at time zero, will no longer be there. The silent space of death will have sucked me in. I will have sunk into the bottomless pit of the past. The words will cease to be mine, and will belong only to the text. My own "I" will be erased, and the "I" of the text will be all that remains of my existence. At that moment, the text will seem as if it exists in a present—but it will only *seem* so. The residue of the past—

14

No, that's not fair to Aarthi.

Genny, go and touch the stretch marks on Aarthi's stomach. I want to kiss your fingertips while they linger there, caressing the roots of time.

0°

Chapter 4

◉ Do you think it is necessary to read the Latin American novels mentioned in this novel?

Yes [ ]   No [ ]

◉ Do you believe this will be an important Tamil novel?

Yes [ ]   No [ ]

(Note: You can wait to answer these questions until after you have finished reading the book.)

◉ Should the author be punished?

Yes [ ]   No [ ]

◉ If yes, how should he be punished?

Expelled from the country   [ ]
Hands chopped off   [ ]
Novel banned   [ ]

◉ Do you think the novel is original?

Yes [ ]   No [ ]

◉ If no, which of the following authors has he plagiarized?

Kosinski   [ ]
Perec   [ ]
Donald Barthelme   [ ]
Ronald Sukenik   [ ]
Italo Calvino   [ ]

◉ Muniyandi says it is not worth reading this novel without first reading Masoch and Marquis de Sade. Do you agree?

Yes [ ]   No [ ]

◉ Who said the following: "I am always thinking about women. But sex is a private matter. I do not write about sex. Sex can be described in dirty words. I do not like dirty words."

Ezra Pound   [ ]
Borges   [ ]
Cortázar   [ ]

◉ How many times do you masturbate in a month?

Nine times   [ ]
More than nine times   [ ]

◉ Who do you fantasize about when you masturbate?

Film star   [ ]
Politician   [ ]
God   [ ]
Beast   [ ]

◉ If beast, which of the following?

Alien beast   [ ]
Serpent   [ ]
Donkey   [ ]
Camel   [ ]
Bull   [ ]
Dog   [ ]
Dolphin   [ ]
Rooster   [ ]
Policeman   [ ]

◉ What do you use to masturbate?

Vibrator   [ ]
Pillow   [ ]
Test-tube   [ ]
Banana   [ ]
Cucumber   [ ]
Brinjal   [ ]
Finger   [ ]
Pen   [ ]
Lathi   [ ]

◉ Have you ever had an orgasm while listening to a percussion instrument?

Yes [ ]   No [ ]

◉ Is there any relation between this novel and these questions?

Yes [ ]   No [ ]

◉ Have you ever had an abortion?

Yes [ ]   No [ ]

◉ Do you support abortion?

Yes [ ]   No [ ]

◉ Have you ever had an orgasm while swinging on a swing?

Yes [ ]   No [ ]

◉ Have you ever had an orgasm while bathing in a waterfall?

Yes [ ]   No [ ]

.

$\boxed{0°}$

Chapter 5

Unsure of what fate they might meet at Muniyandi's hands the words rose up in revolt and lured by the fragrance of the juice of progeny splattered around Muniyandi's bed they slowly approached it tasted it became intoxicated by it then entered Muniyandi's body through his nine orifices and merged with him so that from then on it was the words that were in control of Muniyandi and not the other way round and even though of course from the outside it might seem as though *he* wrote these notes in reality *the words themselves* wrote this novel as is borne out by the fact that the characters attempted to kill the author and in the mayhem that followed the attack a sole character kept protesting with loud cries *the author is not dead the author is not dead* and when the other characters demanded that he prove it he replied *he is merely hiding behind a different name* but none of the other characters believed him and they went away happily saying *it does not matter anymore what Muniyandi was planning to write about us it sure is a good thing that in the first few pages of this novel he was murdered so that now we can write our own futures as we wish them to be* but the lonely character who was sure that Muniyandi was still alive went off searching for him first to Brazil then to Argentina then to the continent of Africa for some time where he lived among the Efé ate elephant meat and kept a journal until he finally realized that Muniyandi was hiding in the character of Nano *if the author who created me is dead then I am dead I have a question about my existence can we create our own existence do I have the necessary skills to do it* we are condemned to live in this world in these pages in this verbal universe up to the 999th page some of us may not see the 999th page may die before the end of this world before the 999th page what then is it the end of the world is it the end of our life no can't be no no it continues in another book no it is suspended it continues in another world

0°

CHAPTER 6

LAST YEAR JALAJASHRI was presented with the award for Best Actress by the President of the nation for her role in a Telugu film the leader of the terrorist party was assassinated by his own party's top cadres Jalajashri also won an award from the Andhra State Government he was arrested on Sunday and brought to the capital where he was killed *Puratchithilakam* the film in which she acted has been selected as the best film of the year this was officially announced by the state on Monday the film was also dubbed in Tamil and released under the title *Puratchithilakam I.P.S.* it became a mega-hit in Tamil Nadu the action force that led the search party arrested the thirty-six year old leader his wife and his children the Foreign Secretary's report said that the army chief claims that he still remains the superstar in spite of being only thirty-six years of age on the other hand we shouldn't forget that she was first introduced in Tamil movies by Kambar Maindhan the movement's leader has been involved in several acts of aggression against the state and is well known to the people of Tamil Nadu Kambar Maindhan's introduction was brought to the capitol for security reasons and interrogated there history tells us that no interrogation has ever failed pledging to eschew violence and espouse ahimsa Radhika Rathi Radha Revathi Ranjini Rekha Renuka Ragini Rajeshwari Rajakumari Rajanala Rajyasri **RAW RAW** the list of **RAW**s is endless he came forward to appeal to the youth through the film *Pullukul*

Kal this request was put forth self-interestedly and although we know it went unnoticed in Tamil Nadu the Foreign Secretary says it was recorded on video after which a squadron of both army soldiers and policemen by *Puratchithilakam I.P.S.* she has become the most popular investigative team to the most secret points of the movement Sridevi and Jayaprada the superstars of yesteryear the movement leader agreed to take to his armory the chief spot that was the centre for both the movement and its armory were renowned character actors that informed his politburo member to remove the important files and information after Jayasudha Sridevi and Jayapradha moved on to the Hindi film world for greater glamour and submitted to the investigative team Radha Banupriya and the various other leaders who would not accept the move unexpectedly for character roles Jayasudha suddenly pulled out the gun was the situation today and these women shot down and the various leaders are wanted by the army be it glamour sex or heroic performance and is shot dead after which an emergency whatever the role under heavy security those elder leaders' bodies swimming in success is Jalajashri were cremated reported the foreign secretary the leader of the movement Jalajashri to receive her award assassination there should be an extensive investigation ordered the Police Inspector General, and left.

0°

Chapter 7

THE WORD IS WRITING itself with other words.

He's copulating with his own shadow. Here, smell my word. Can you smell my blood in it? Can you taste it?

Can you put forth the whole of your experience, without censoring anything?

Will you make me a gift of your poem? Can you tuck it into a tiny little package, like a nuclear oven?

She wants to record your life. Just a few passages of it.

I shivered, and I transformed my shivering into a kiss for you.

You shivered as well, and you said your shivers were your poems.

Many laborers gave up their lives in protest against Draco's 9th century A.D. law making the stealing of grapes punishable by death.

Words swim about meaninglessly, like empty vessels bobbing in the water.

I ache for your touch.

A solider, assigned to guard a ruined fort on a lonely island, is slowly losing his mind.

Girls bunk school and gather flowers.

The word dies, even as it is being written.

The poet dies, even as he is ignored by the multitude.

Neruda is visiting the ruins of the Inca capital, Machu Pichu, in the Andes mountains above Cusco, Peru.

Rilke asks, **My soul, dressed in silence, rises up and stands alone before you. Can't you see?**

I'm writing. What else can I do besides write? I'm dying. What else can I do besides die? Etc. etc.

Evil is hidden inside good. Good is hidden inside evil.

Writing is not about life, writing is just about writing.

Neither nature nor art means anything apart from itself. They simply are. Why couldn't *I* have written that, instead of Robbes-Grillet?

We no longer look at the world with the eyes of a confessor, of a doctor, or of God himself (all significant hypotheses of the classical novelist), but with the eyes of a man walking in his city with no other horizon than the scene before him, no other power than that of his own eyes. How can I make any sense of Roland Barthes?

He is sitting alone on Mount Road. Sunday evening. Lacking human company. Confused about where to head next. Go back to the room and read? It's difficult to decide. He watches the smoke rings as he exhales.

How many slaves are buried under the Great Wall of China?

A man and a woman are writing a poem together with their blood.

It is impossible to write with words. They slip away even as I write them down. If I manage to catch them, they melt.

Hands extend from an asylum window.

A beggar sleeps under a neem tree on a river bank.

A tiny feather brushes against an earlobe.

A magician threads an elephant through the eye of a needle.

A silence hangs over Connaught Place Ring Road on an autumn morning.

A reader asks: "Why do all actresses have pet dogs?" The editor responds with: "Because the actresses' husbands' tongues are not long enough."

On the island of Lesbos, **Sappho** is writing down the first ever mention of lesbians.

An editor of a popular journal cuts the word *asshole* from the short story a writer sent in.

"Erase the difference between me and you," says Cioux.

A fat actress, with a stomach like a pumpkin, hands like gourds, and thighs like the two halves of a split pig, is advertising soap products on the television.

Words on the walls of a prison, on the walls of an asylum, on the walls of public toilets; words on school desks, on condom boxes, in textbooks, on a judge's judgment sheet, in university corridors, on city buses, in the mouth of a policeman who's high on zarda beeda, in the prime minister's diary; words scattered all over the place like this; a little girl gathers them up, now she goes to sell them at the ironsmith's shop; who is that now, walking around in her dream? Come on now, Mr. Roland Barthes, please, stay out of there.

0°

CHAPTER 8

The following is Ninth-Century-A.D.-Dead-Brain's review of Muniyandi's book:

The most completely absurd feature of this book is its attempt to equate common thieves with revolutionaries. Muniyandi does not seem to grasp the difference between righteous rebellion and everyday poverty-driven crime. It appears that, having read somewhere that the revolt by the Santhal tribe against the moneylenders later turned into an uprising against the British, Muniyandi has modeled the climax of his novel after these events, and believes that this gives his work revolutionary credentials. But Muniyandi's "revolutionaries" do not stop at looting banks. They also loot textile showrooms and kill policemen.

The "revolutionary" hero, Mayta, seems to me to be a mere burglar. I fail to see how his protest is motivated by any ideology.

I once treated Muniyandi to a quarter-bottle of whiskey and chicken biryani at Sriramalinga Vilas, and we gossiped generally about the literary scene. In a drunken emotional state, he let slip that he had stolen the idea of modeling non-fictional documentary narrative on older historical events from *Tres Tristes Tigres*, by Guillermo Cabrera Infante.

The hero of Muniyandi's story is Mayta. (What kind of a name is this? What language is it? Maybe Muniyandi would have done better if he had gone ahead and written his novel in this strange foreign tongue, rather than in Tamil.) Mayta and his textile-showroom-looting friends have been cleverly depicted as modern-day Santhal revolutionaries. If we accept this comparison, then we must also accept that when all those government clerks who travel by the 27C from Anna Nagar to the Secretariat for work and jot down stories for small time journals in their spare time start picking the pockets of their fellow passengers on the bus, they can claim that their actions are not shameful, but rather a form of protest against the imperialism of America and the IMF.

Muniyandi boasts that his novel is based on real events. To investigate the truth behind it all, I traveled to the location of those events, along with a friend of mine from Nagercoil. We met some women carrying pots of water, and questioned them. This is what we learned. A few unemployed youths had started talking about Mao and his revolution, and eventually decided to go and loot a tiny 18' x 9' textile shop for a mere four hundred forty-one rupees. *This* is the stupid incident that Muniyandi is comparing to the Santhal revolt. The poor shop owner, Paalvannam Pillai, is a father of six daughters and three sons.

After I finished my investigation and was on my way to the liquor shop, the police inspector who had come along as my traveling companion stopped at a certain place, took out his handkerchief, dabbed at his eyes, and blew his nose. I could tell these were no crocodile tears, nothing like the fake outpourings of sympathy for prostitutes and lepers with which Muniyandi has filled his book. It was clear that my friend's grief was real, and so I asked him the reason for it. Apparently, this was the spot where his colleague, while in pursuit of the thieves, had tripped on a stone, fell, cracked the back of his skull, and died. I stared at the stone. What an absurd world this is, I thought; it was like something from Albert Camus' *The Stranger*. I thought I could hear the stone whispering something: that all Muniyandi's lies, wrapped up in a disguise of Marxism and structuralism, were falling apart.

Muniyandi's version of the tale is this. After the bank robbery attempt failed, Mayta and his friends took to their heels. The plainclothes policemen and villagers chased after them, throwing stones. Even though Mayta had an AK-45, he would not shoot back at them, for fear of hurting the innocent villagers, and so the band of "revolutionaries" was stoned to death. With these lies Muniyandi attempts to paint his hero as some great humanist, and get his readers to sniff their noses and shed tears for a false rebel.

But here is the story I uncovered. Even while they were still inside the bank, a fight broke out between Mayta's friends and the bank cashier, and Mayta *did* use his gun. This is proved by the fact that the cashier is still on medical leave. There are also several bullet holes in the walls. Somehow, in all that commotion (do you really expect me to call it an "uprising"?) nobody died; Muniyandi sees this as evidence of humanitarianism, but to me, it seems to indicate nothing more than that Mayta and his gang members had spectacularly lousy aim.

In any case, I will relate the rest of what actually happened. The villagers chased them, in spite of the gun. They even threw stones at the thieves. Mayta aimed his AK-45 at a few brave-hearted young villagers who, determined not to let the bandits escape, started to pounce on them. Even as his finger was feeling for the trigger, a stone fired from a maravan's slingshot hit poor Mayta right in the eyes. Blood poured out, and he was put to death by the following volley of stones. Seeing the demise of their leader, the gang went berserk and tried to fire their rifles—which, as we know, failed to work.

According to the villagers, it was the divine grace of Nagercoil Velikkaruppan that prevented the gang's guns from firing and changing the course of history.

0°

MUNIYANDI'S STORY

SHE IS ON HER WAY somewhere when she passes a temple. On the street corner, preparations are underway for the idol to be paraded through the streets. There are chrysanthemum garlands. She decides to sit down in the crowd to watch, when some other woman starts talking about a dead body in the dumpster. A young child immediately takes a look, gets frightened, and runs off, bare legs flashing. *If there's been a death near the temple, then the procession will be stopped,* she reasons, and gets up to go home. She puts down whatever it is she has in her hand, and, hearing a thud, looks down to see the dead child. As she looks at it, its eyes open; its limbs start to twitch; it begins to cry. *It must have gone mad,* she thinks, and takes hold of its neck, intending to strangle it, but doesn't have the heart. The man comes, shouts something, seems to come to some decision, and leaves in a hurry. She is frozen again, staring blankly at the child. Now the child's limbs start to take on strange shapes; they become the limbs of a snail, a gecko, a tortoise, a lizard, a spider, a snake, a scorpion, a leech, a fish. She brings the broom and dustpan; as she sweeps up the mess, it transforms into a wriggling cluster of worms. Trying to control her disgust, she goes out and dumps it in the dumpster.

Puchi, lying uncontrollably drunk at the side of the road, climbs up and leans over the edge of the dumpster to puke, but sees the stiff body of the child and recoils in terror. The child's stomach has been gnawed at by a rat that now lurks in the corner of the bin. *A girl child is always useful for earning an income,* thinks Puchi, so he brings it to Neena, who, on seeing the child, beats Puchi black and blue. "Are you so drunk you can't even tell the difference between a boy and a girl?" Neena demands. She takes the child to a doctor. Though it has been lying in the dumpster in the cold, chewed by rats, for nearly the whole thirty-six hours since its birth, the child survives.

And so, eighteen thousand million years after the world came into being, this child, born in the month of Margazhi, has survived to become a sentence on this page. All due to Neena and Puchi.

Colostrum The yellow liquid that a mother's breast lactates for a few days after delivery. It **contains a lot of proteins and vitamins. It has antibodies against many common diseases especially those that the mother has had earlier.** These **antibodies** from the mother's breast milk protect the child until it is capable of generating **antibodies** on its own.

Eating ice cream causes throat infection, and may even require surgery. Bombay sweets are made of fish gills. Bombay sweet sellers usually come around booming a horn. Kids buy the sticky sweets in various shapes—fish, wristwatches, planes, ships—and watch them till they begin to sweat and melt in the heat of the sun. The sweets are shaped with spit.

Dear Lady Reader, you should also know how Muniyandi converted to existentialism. When he was in his adolescence—perhaps even earlier—and already thirsting to become a writer, he began to imbibe all the reading material he could lay his hands on. He read Einstein, Brihadharnyaka's commentary on the *Upanishads*, Kurumbur Kuppusami, Gramsci, Ambedkar, *Manu Shastra*, the *Mahabharatam*, *The Arabian Nights*, Robert Musil, pig genetics, Aandal, Che Guevara, Alejo Carpentier, body politics, the history of Bolivia, biographies of mountain trekkers, criminal statements, innumerable love letters, the geology of volcanic landforms, marine biology, legends about pilgrimage sites, **Gershom Scholem**, René Descartes—the list went on and on. Eventually he came across an interview with Parveen Babi in which she declared that she was an existentialist. At first, Muniyandi had trouble pronouncing the word. He said it aloud to himself several times, then looked it up in the dictionary. He immediately fell in love with the meaning, and proclaimed that he, Muniyandi, was an existentialist. "I am an existentialist," he wrote in his notebook, over and over again, loving the word more and more each time. His English lecturer happened to notice this while looking over his notes. **"Are you an existentialist?"** she asked him. Muniyandi stood up and replied shyly, "Yes, Ma'am."

A landowner in Suththa, a village in the state of Bihar, shot down a nine-year-old boy, reportedly because the boy had stolen a Petromax lantern from the landowner's house. Muniyandi did not know who his birth parents were, but he did know his foster mother was a sex worker. He was never ashamed about this fact; still, he made no mention of it in his autobiography. In a village in Mirzapur District, near Kalipur, the husband of a woman named Mira Bai borrowed a hundred eighty rupees from a carpet-maker. Ananthasami, having done some research on Muniyandi's neighborhood and the street's cottage industry, exposed the lie to the public in his review of the autobiography, saying that although Muniyandi had deliberately tried to hide his mother's profession and present her has a woman of great chastity, he had failed miserably in the attempt. Since he was unable to pay back the loan, his family became bonded laborers to the carpet-maker. I took this matter to the court, with the help of the Children's Freedom Association in that district. As hard as Muniyandi tried, he could not come up with a reason why he had not revealed the truth about his mother. The court decided that Mira Bai's son Umashankar, age nine, should be awarded thirty-six thousand rupees in compensation for having been forced to work as the carpet-maker's slave. All through his childhood, Muniyandi had slept under his mother's cot. But with the complicity of the local police, the carpet-maker managed not only to avoid paying the amount, but also to have Umashankar's elder brother—a bonded laborer as well—arrested on false charges. But he wouldn't start out there; when the lights were switched off, he would drop off to sleep next to his mother. The boys and Mira Bai's husband received a thrashing from the police. He could only go to sleep with his head resting on his mother's chest, listening to the rhythm of her heart. They were warned that they would be dismembered if they ever spoke about it publicly. The *lub-dub* sound, the way her breast rose and fell, gave him the comforting feeling of a long train journey. I also saw for myself that thousands of children were working in the stone quarries in Faridabad. Otherwise, he would toss and turn, but never really fall asleep. The Association's Pakistan branch reports that there are ninety lakh child bonded laborers in that country. The rhythm of her heart and her warm embrace would lull him to sleep in spite of his hunger. Most of them were employed in brick factories. But on waking up, he would find himself under the cot.

Ninety young men were killed and thrown into the Ganga. It is that same sound that woke me up several times at night. Because Kuchi Devi's husband refused to lend his wife to his employer, he was burned alive. When he woke up for the first time like that, he could not understand why he was under the cot or make sense of the strange noises coming from above, so he rolled out, and saw a dark shape moving up and down on top of his mother. It was only then that he began to understand what was going on. She was pregnant then. When he was slightly older, he tried doing the same thing those dark shapes had done to his mother to the neighbor's daughter and her mother happened to see it and started screaming and because of that his mother and her mother had a huge fight where they tore at each other's hair and rolled around in the streets. Because the local police refused to register Kuchi Devi's case, she came to Delhi. Since that day, whenever someone came to see my mother, I would go out. *Maa aapsanket karte hain, to me upne kamre ke jhoothe banaata houn.* The room he called home was only three by six feet, so he had no other option. The 1980 census report says that there are 180 lakhs of child laborers. They had to bathe and shit on the streets. They work in factories, hotels, cinema halls and small shops. They do not cook. They roll beedis. They break stones. They work the night shifts in hotels and glass factories. Even now Misra is surprised. Most of the employees in these factories are children. If they wanted to shit in the day, where could Amma—or any other woman—go? The temperature in the factory was 40.5 degrees centigrade. I have seen my mother, and other women too, go off before dawn with a small pot of water to the open ground across the road. 72% of India's matchboxes are manufactured in Sivakasi. How many children there are, working from dawn to dusk in these factories! *"Arrey bachche, teri maa kithar gayee?"* asked a customer. The Indian Industries Act says that children should not be put to work more than 270 minutes daily. It was then that I began learning English. Yet they are forced to work throughout the day. **"My mother is funking,"** said Misra to the customer. From that day onwards, the other children called Misra **funky funky funky**.

0°

IF ANYONE ASKED Fuckrunissa how many rooms were there in the huge mansion—*palace* might be a better word—she would just shrug.

"Who knows? You think I have nothing better to do than to count them all?" she would ask, wearily, but with just a touch of pride.

For the mansion belonged to her. It really did have an extraordinary number of bedrooms, as well as a swimming pool at the side, a few ballrooms, and a row of servants' quarters behind the building for the horse cart drivers, palanquin bearers (Fuckrunissa preferred to travel in a palanquin—she hated horse chariots), cooks, punkawallahs, washerwomen, and other sundry maids. Behind these quarters was the garage for the palanquin and the horse shed.

As if this was not enough, Nawab Mirza Ali Khan wanted to have a canal dug from the Yamuna River to the garden of the fort, so that fishermen could row right up to the doorstep to provide them with the freshest fish. Just imagine!

Out of all the women in his zamin, the Nawab's love was only for Fuckrunissa. She knew that no other could take her place in his heart.

In the beginning, before he understood her character, the Nawab kept asking Fuckrunissa to come and join his harem. But she refused.

If she were to go and live there, Fuckrunissa thought, she would vanish, become subsumed. She had not been born for such a fate. "Nawab Sahib, I am your slave," she told him. "All of us here in the zamin are your slaves. We go wherever you order us to go. But we have grown up as wild parrots, breathing the free, open air of your land. Please, do not cage us in your harem. I was born with bells on my feet—I cannot be walled in." Hearing such eloquent speech, the Nawab was eventually convinced.

There was a particular night when Fuckrunissa gave an enchanting recital of ghazals and dancing, and those in the audience claimed that they had never before enjoyed such a musical feast. The Nawab, with his poet's heart, felt the same. He melted in the romance of her voice that night.

"How do you come to be so talented, woman?" asked the Nawab. "Women from royal households, who have studied for years under the best teachers, cannot match you."

"Fuckrunissa must have enjoyed that life, Misra," said Neena.

"Oh, I disagree. How can you say that? Wasn't it after reading her diary that you decided to give up your hedonistic lifestyle and get married?"

But Misra was wrong about Fuckrunissa. She loved every instant of her life in the fort. In her diary, she wrote pages about her teacher Maulvi Nizamudeen, and about his lessons on aquatic dance, astronomy, philosophy and logic.

The Maulvi was a great linguist who knew Arabic, Persian, Hebrew and Greek. He had read all the great epics and mythologies. But his direct experience of the world had taught him more than all the books ever could.

"It was only after reading some of the stories the Maulvi told Fuckrunissa that I began to take an interest in my own sexuality," said Neena.

The Maulvi told me the story of a dove who, having lost its partner, picked up a stone in its beak, flew up as high as it could, swallowed the stone, and then dropped to the ground to crash and die.

"'Brother, when you brought Mandodhari here, I was so overjoyed I kissed you. When you made the strings of your veena sing with that joy, I traveled along with you through that ecstatic musical space. But Brother, you have now become old. You have grown children. To have abducted Seetha, at this age, is not right,' said the younger brother to the elder. But Ravanan did not pay heed. So his younger brother left him, and took refuge with the epic hero Raman.

It was then that Raman narrated the dove story to explain the concept of self-sacrifice," said the Maulvi in his soft voice.

A hunter, tired and hungry because he had not found any game, came to lie down under a tree. He gathered some dry twigs, and lit a fire to keep warm. In the tree was a pair of doves. "Darling," the male dove told the female, "that hunter, lying there below us, is hungry because he has not found any game. It is our duty to save him. Therefore, I shall drop into his fire, to become his meal. But if he is still not satiated, then you, too, must fall into the fire."

Delirious with hunger, the hunter ate the male dove. The female watched him. When it was clear that he was still hungry, she fell into the fire as well.

Our town is full of doves; there are more doves here than in any other town in the world. If other towns are full of air, then ours is full of the air exhaled by doves. I think God has sent the doves so that man may forget his sorrows. I wish, from the bottom of my heart, that I had been born as a dove.

Do you know why there are so many doves? It is because Hazrat Abdul Qadri Owliya is buried here. He was a Sufi saint who came to India two hundred and seventy years ago. There are many legends about him. His good works were innumerable; he cured every disease in the area and brought people back to life who had been bitten by snakes. Everyone in the town, both children and adults, knows the story of how he and his disciples crossed the river, and could narrate the events as though they happened yesterday.

There was a great flood; the raging river had overflowed. Nobody could figure out how to get across to the opposite bank. Owliya shut his eyes and began chanting the *Sura Fatiha*, and when he finished the chant, he and his disciples were standing on the other shore. There was another miraculous story, about the way he saved the life of Hamidha Banu, the daughter of Nawab Ali Mansur, the ruler of the land in those days. The nawab loved his daughter more than his own life. Suddenly, she disappeared. She was not the kind of girl who would go out on her own without informing her father. They searched everywhere but could not find her. So he came to Hazrat Abdul Qadri Owliya for help. Owliya poured some water into a bowl, and asked the Nawab to gaze into it. There, in the water, he saw his beloved daughter, her hands and feet bound, on the back of a galloping horse. She had been kidnapped by Mushtaq Ahmed, son of Umar Sheik, the king of the neighboring land. It was also revealed that the Nawab's own Chief Minister had assisted in her abduction. The Nawab threw his minister in prison, gathered his soldiers, and thanks to Owliya's grace, was able to rescue his daughter.

Perhaps it is due to the presence of Owliya's dargah in this town that the Hindu-Muslim riots that so often plague the neighboring states never seem to occur here. Elsewhere, there were riots because a temple was being constructed in the kasbah; riots because the Muslim landlords kept borrowing from the Hindu moneylenders; riots because a cow's head was thrown into a temple, in retribution for a slaughtered pig that had been thrown into a masjid; riots because a kabadi match was lost. Only when the white soldiers arrived would the rioters be brought under control; and only after peace had returned would anyone ever come to know of it here, in this town. But always, before the soldiers arrived, several people would be killed. Whenever Fuckrunissa heard stories like this, she would wonder how a man could kill another.

Fuckrunissa was almost nine years old when she first encountered death. She would never forget that day. She had come to the dargah to feed the doves, as usual. There, from a distance, she saw a white dove which had hurt its wing and was hopping around in pain. Before she could run over to help it, the dove was run down by a speeding horse chariot. Fuckrunissa came running to pick it up; as she cradled it in her palms, it heaved its last breath, and she felt death for the first time, right there at her fingertips.

She had asked the Maulvi: "Why do living things die?" "Such is the law of nature," the Maulvi had replied. The answer had not satisfied her. Here were men killing their fellow men—and in the name of religion! To whom should she go now, for explanation?

But of course, it must be by the grace of Owliya that such incidents have never occurred in *this* zamin. As long as his grace persists, there is no need for soldiers or sentries to guard this fort.

Fuckrunissa's diary went on and on like this. Scattered in between were notes on her dance compositions and Urdu poems. Until the moment when Nawab Mirza surrendered to the British, Fuckrunissa devoted herself to the Nawab's pleasure. He in turn was enslaved by her Urdu poems and ghazals. Then there were pages and pages about smoking opium from the hookah. She writes about an occasion when the Nawab was too overcome with emotion to speak, and about rubbing opium onto his lips, and reviving him with tea.

"Whenever I think of Fuckrunissa," Neena said, *"I imagine the hookah, its gadagadagada noise, and the enveloping smell of the smoke."*

But the charms of the hookah, and of Fuckrunissa's beautiful voice, were all brought to an end by the military power and cunning tactics of the British. The Nawab, though he could smell the most subtle nuances in the scent of a jasmine flower, and appreciate all the finer points of Fuckrunissa's dancing, was not smart enough to negotiate with the British. He depended for defense upon a bunch of soldiers too lost in their wine and their women to offer any real resistance. And so, the Nawab was killed, and his palace looted. Afterwards the white soldiers' eyes turned to Fuckrunissa's mansion. They took everything, leaving only the roof and walls. Kashmiri shawls, Persian carpets, bejewelled wine glasses, the ruby-studded hookahs, the diamond-encrusted spittoons; they took them all, not leaving a single thing behind.

Fuckrunissa crushed a diamond into powder and swallowed it, thus giving up her life. The women who had depended on her for employment had no other option but to go to the streets and sell their bodies. All of them, including Fuckrunissa's adopted daughter, Neena, contracted venereal diseases, which they then spread among the white soldiers. Once alerted to the danger, the whites made a law forcing the women to register and have their bodies checked out at regular intervals. Their income was taxed, as well. Thus the women of the Nawab's harem were reduced to street prostitutes.

Neena did not like that life. She fell in love. Her lover promised to marry her. It was only after the marriage, when she entered his home, did she understand:

I have been brought as a slave to his house. He and a huge army of relatives, his parents, their parents, his father's younger brother, his elder brother and his wife, and a few cows, have all been waiting here for me to come and serve them.

She had to get up before dawn to milk the cows. Make tea when the rest of the household woke up—some of them wanted milk instead. Then make the chapathis. Wash all their clothes. Make the cowdung into dung cakes. (Here, Didi would offer her some help, but not with anything else.) Sweep the entire house. The old hag—his father's mother—would pee in the bed. She would have to wash the room. Change the sheets.

Every time she looked at the old hag, she wondered if God had forgotten to send the Reaper out for her. Wash the dishes. She herself would be half dead before she could get a shine on the brass spittoons, into which they had been spitting their betelnut juice throughout the day. Dinner. After dinner, massage the legs of the women of the house. Do the dishes. Clean the kitchen. Sometimes, massage the hag with mustard oil, and bathe her. "Jilay Singh is lucky to get a woman like you, Beti," the hag would say, caressing Neena's face and then cracking her knuckles to ward off the evil eye. It wasn't only the hag. Everyone in the house would go on and on like that: "Beti, please massage my body." "Beti, please give me my bath." "Boil the milk and soak some *jalebis* in it, Beti." "Dear child, we don't know whether we are bound for heaven or for hell, but *you* will definitely go to heaven!"

It was a different sort of problem from the men. I was making dung cakes, after finishing the chapathis, when Jilay Singh's father came and carried me off. When I objected, Jilay Singh said, "Look here, Neena. In this family, we know the names of our forefathers going back four generations. Do you even know the names of your parents? If you had stayed out there on the streets, you would have had—what, say nine men a day? In a month, 270. In a year, 3240. If you worked for eighteen years, just count how many you would have had to serve. What is it you're lacking here? We treat you like a queen. We eat what you feed us. What more do you want?"

The next day the old man came again. I objected vehemently. The entire household surrounded us. "Beti is possessed," said the old hag. Nobody listened to my protests. Instead they bound my hands in chains. The exorcist was brought in. My sari was ripped off and he threw me naked on the sand. "Arrey, Beti! Arrey, Beti!" sobbed the old hag. I went limp. My lips whispered for water. The exorcist took me inside the room and fucked me like a beast. Consciousness and unconsciousness came and went. When I struggled to stay awake, I could tell that the man on top of me was not the exorcist, but someone else. Before I could recognize who it was, I would slip again into blackness.

It was only after I became fully conscious that I realized every man in that household had taken me in turn to drive out the evil spirit. After that, I had to go any time they beckoned. That old man—what arrogance! Whenever he caught me alone, he would stuff his organ into my mouth and nearly suffocate me. I would think: God, if You really are there, You should be made to go through this torture too.

There was no way to escape. But I did not accept defeat so easily. I spat on their food, pissed on it, threw bits of pussy crust into the potato fry. They spied on me, and saw me do it. The exorcist was brought in again. This time the exorcism was violent. I had to eat my own excrement. My genitals were stuffed with chili powder. "You are torturing our Neena! Wait, I shall take away your clitoris," the exorcist said, and pulled out the devil's clitoris and sliced it off with his knife. Then he rammed a huge stick into the devil's vagina.

I was unconscious for several days. They drugged me heavily. I could hear them sobbing "Beti, Beti!" all around me. I am back in Fuckrunissa's palace… Nissa's palace, sitting with my left foot folded under me and my right leg a gopuram, smoking the hookah. The room is filled with opium fumes. Gada gada gada gada gada gada gada gada gada. After the smoke, I sing; but it is Nissa's voice. Nissa and I play tag. She teaches me to swim in the pool. I lie down with my cheek caressing the cold marble. The stone slowly turns warm against my cheek… Nissa's cheek.

I was lucky to come out of it alive. The devil which had possessed me fell away with my rotted uterus; they said it would never return. I don't know how long I lay there, limp as a string. All I know is that, having survived, I was a different person.

I stayed quiet. Summer came, and brought unbearable heat. The air became thick and heavy. The winds would swirl the burning sands into a demonic serpent and raise it up to the sky. Whatever lay in the serpent's path, whether a tree, a cow, or a man, it would be torn to pieces. The year before, a cow belonging to the house had been killed in just such a tornado; it was caught in the vortex, and the head was ripped off and flung away into the distance. There was no way to know when the breeze would turn threatening, lift the sands of the desert and throw them at the face. There was always sandy grit between the teeth. The old women would all cover their faces, but I was not allowed to; Jilay Singh said my face was like the crescent moon, and he wanted to be able to see it all the time.

It was during that summer that I finally managed to escape. A sandstorm came; the members of the household were all tired and asleep. I tucked a knife into my waistband. I pressed a pillow over each woman's face in turn, killing them painlessly.

The men slept alone, so it was even easier. Jilay Singh's brother was sleeping in his room; I dropped a huge stone pestle on his head. I didn't even turn to look back at him. His uncle was sleeping in the courtyard. I slowly placed my hand on his organ. He woke up, saw me, and started gabbering something unintelligible, as though he was seeing a ghost. I didn't waste any time; I cut off his organ with my knife. Jilay Singh, who had been sleeping outside, heard him scream and came running in. He took my arm and twisted it behind my back. The knife slipped out of my hand. As he bent down to pick it up, I chomped down hard on his organ with my teeth. He hit me on the head, again and again, but I didn't let go; the beating only made me bite harder. Finally I bit it off completely, and spat it out. He fell over like an uprooted tree.

I wanted to do the same thing to the old man, so I came outside. He was lying there with his mouth open. I approached him, and placed my hand on his organ. It was cold. Uncomprehending, I tried to shake him awake. But he was already dead.

Not wanting to commit suicide, I wandered here and there… until I met Shireen.

Shireen, Shireen, Shireen! Do you know who she is? She is my Goddess! How bright her eyes are! A quiet light of inner peace. A light that shines right through to your marrow. A look from her, like a glimpse of the moon, thrills the body like a cascading waterfall.

I have seen such a serene light once before, in an emerald that Nissa had. That light would speak to you. It would warm your heart, caress you, kiss your eyelashes, place you on a tree swing and swing you up into the clouds, pluck the stars out to play pallangkuzhi with you, spread out the sky before you as a carpet, take you into the deep sea and show you all the underwater wonders, introduce you to the land of the mermaids, play games with you beyond the orbits of the planets, teach you secret ways of escaping from sea dragons.

I have preserved that light within me, preserved it so that it will never be lost in the tornado. It is tucked safely within the sky blanket she gave me.

"Darling Neena, come, I shall gift you that light"—those were Shireen's last words. The person who loved me is dead.

She was the one who taught me dance and music. Everyone in the fort loved the thumris I sang. These were what she gave me. They were hers.

I was disgusted with men. Her beauty protected me from the men who visited our fort. If any men came to me, enthralled by my thumris, I would show my scars and chase them off. If any still persisted, Shireen would charm them away.

She pressed her spit into every wound on my body. I can say truthfully there is not a spot on my body that she has not kissed.

The fragrance of her body thrilled me. Her lips sparked an erotic fire. Her spit and her cum gave me back my life. She licked me from the tip of my big toe to my foot, to my calves, to my knees, to my thighs, to my waist, to my navel, to my stomach, to my nipples, to my neck, to my shoulders, to my eyebrows, to my cheeks, to my nose, to my eyelashes—her snakelike tongue would suddenly enter my yoni.

I shuddered with pleasure. Shireen, Shireen!

Shireen died holding my hands. The intense meditation had come to an end.

You will not believe this: her spirit left her through my hands. I felt the life slipping out of her and into my body through my fingers. Shireen had not died; she had merged into me.

It was on the day that Shireen died that Puchi brought me the child from the garbage bin. In its tiny body, gnawed by a rat, there was still life trembling. Even now, I am amazed that I could help it survive.

0°

CHAPTER 9

IN HIS REVIEW of Muniyandi's novel, Ninth-Century-A.D.-Dead-Brain has woven in accounts of various events that occurred in different times and different places. I am going to give you some more facts about those events now; listen.

Firstly, the bomb attack in the textile showroom. Paalvannam Pillai, the showroom owner, is not merely a textile showroom owner. He also owns many of the beedi factories in the villages of Seenur, Vanjur, and Kaarasamangalam. You should come and see these villages. The total population here is 13,500, of which 72% work rolling beedis. In your town, people begin registering their children for pre-kindergarten and lower kindergarten even before they turn thirty-six months old. Some of them even send letters to the editors of English dailies complaining that they have to pay a fee to register and retain a school seat as soon as the child is born. But in these villages, the children are pledged to the beedi factories when they are only thirty-six months old. A woman who was widowed at a young age and left with three young kids reports that she has mortgaged her children for 1800 and 900 rupees. The youngest is still a babe-in-arms. The beedi factory is a dark stuffy dungeon. Stop reading at this point and visualize a dark, stuffy dungeon for a moment. In each room there are nine children toiling from dawn until nine in the night. There is a short lunch break. If they manage to roll 900 beedis they get a daily wage of eighteen rupees. The children who work as bonded laborers get only nine rupees. They are whipped with wires to make them work faster. The girl children bear the pain; the boys attempt to flee. But if these run-away boys are caught, their limbs are bound to poles with thick chains. They are released only if they promise to obey—and even then only during work hours. During the lunch break, and while being taken home, they remain bound. They also have to do domestic chores in the owner's house and construction work when ordered. A girl bonded laborer works at the construction site, but her elder brother has run off, unable to bear the torture. Still, Paalvannam Pillai claims the factory supervisors do not torment the children. He also insists that the parents send their children here only to be trained in a skill, and that he plays music on a tape deck so that the children do not feel burdened by the work. Most beedi laborers don't get anything to eat, and survive only on tea. Children are pledged so the parents can meet wedding expenses, or visit the Sabarimalai temple. I do not want to write about this anymore. I'm tired of it. That bank robbery is now history. Ninth-Century-A.D.-Dead-Brain won't be able to make sense of any of this anyway. It looks as though if Dead-Brain could find an Aryan yoni, he would stop worrying about such things.

$0°$

NINTH-CENTURY-A.D.-DEAD-BRAIN'S STORY

NINTH-CENTURY-A.D.-DEAD-BRAIN roams the Earth as an immortal, just as Aswathaman from the *Mahabharatam* is immortal. He was born in the 9th century A.D., and ever since then, his male organ has been growing non-stop. Next to his organ, the organs of Sornamuthu Pillai and New York Karuppan are like tiny specks of dust. You do know the story of Sornamuthu Pillai, don't you, Lady Reader? No? Then I shall tell it to you now.

Sornamuthu Pillai had to undergo surgery on his male organ. The nurse who attended him during the surgery noticed something strange; the organ bore a tattoo, green letters which formed the word SOLLAI. The nurse could hardly contain her curiosity. Finally, on the day of his discharge, reasoning that he was, after all, a very old man, she drummed up the courage to ask him, hesitantly: "I saw something written on your... please don't take this the wrong way, but... can you tell me what it means?"

"Phoo, is that all you've been worrying about?" he replied. "Please don't take this the wrong way, but... just kindly touch it with your hand, and you'll see." She did, and when the huge organ swelled, the tattoo read SORNAMUTHU PILLAI.

48

Similarly, New York Karuppan had a tattoo on his organ that read WENDY. When a woman shyly asked him, "Is Wendy the name of your girlfriend?" he too asked her to touch it, and when it swelled to its full size it read WELCOME TO NEW YORK, HAVE A NICE DAY.

But Ninth-Century-A.D.-Dead-Brain's dick is so big I could write the entire text of *0°* on it. The organ had been growing for so many centuries, and the foreskin had become so thick and gnarled, that it now resembled a wild creeper vine. People who saw him for the first time took him for a mendicant roaming the jungle with a knotted vine wrapped around his shoulders. Nobody suspected it was his dick. Still, many tales and fanciful stories were told about him among the young men, though none of them had seen him. To relate all of these tales would take up more space than available in this volume, so I shall give you the following as a sample.

This story is about a girl who became particularly terrified after hearing the stories about Ninth-Century-A.D.-Dead-Brain. She was phallophobic, and therefore had sworn she would never get married. Her mother, of course, was worried, and kept pestering her daughter to marry. Unable to put up with her nagging, the girl agreed, but with a condition.

"The groom should not have *that*."

"What di? What shouldn't he have?"

"*That* only, Amma, *that* only! Don't ask me anything more, I feel shy!"

N.C.A.D.D.-Brain, who had never been married in his several centuries of life, who had never even had sex, whose long search for an Aryan yoni had proven unsuccessful, came to know about this girl and presented himself to the mother hoping that this match, at least, might work out. The mother looked at the tall strong savage, with his untamed beard and the thick vine around his shoulders. She told him about the girl's condition. "I know, madam; I do not have *that*," N.C.A.D.D.-Brain lied coolly.

"So you may say, but I need to check for myself," said the mother, and felt below his waist, between his thighs. She could feel his balls, but not *that*.

On the nuptial night, even though the mother had checked between the groom's thighs, the daughter was still scared. "Mummy, mummy," she begged, "please come and lie beside me!" Knowing about her daughter's phobia, the mother lay next to the girl on the nuptial bed; worn out after the long wedding ceremony, she fell asleep almost immediately. The girl, not completely rid of her fears, was tossing and turning in bed. N.C.A.D.D.-Brain, of course, could not even shut his eyes. He lay staring at the ceiling, cursing his fate. But his organ was not bothered about his distress. Feeling the warmth of the women next to it, it began to slither over the thighs of the girl, who screamed that she was being attacked by a snake. At the sound of her scream the mother woke up to find a huge warm serpent resting on her thighs as well, and began to thrash away at it. It wasn't until much later that they understood the true nature of that serpent.

Ninth-Century-A.D.-Dead-Brain, having thus been beaten by both the mother and the daughter, was frustrated in his efforts. He spent some time in the literary scene before meeting Kulla Chithan, who became his dear friend. Kulla Chithan is an expert in black magic who wanders the forest in search of rare herbs and plays with skulls in the funeral ghat. He once gave Ninth-Century-A.D.-Dead-Brain a rare palm-leaf manuscript on which was written the secret of charming women, which read as follows:

Grind together bones from the funeral pyre and the juice of the musu-musukai, pour it into the egg of a black hen that has been pierced at the top and had the white removed from it, wrap the egg in a cloth, and bury it in a cobra's burrow for forty-five days. Then remove it, break off the shell, add the meat of a male dog, then on a copper plate etch the mystical diagrams shown; chant the words for nine days while fanning the mixture with the smoke of burning neem leaves; then on the ninth day, go to the east end of town and put the mixture in your mouth.

நீ	கா	ன	டி	க	ர	தை	து	உ
க	எ	ண	கொ	ன	பு	ய	ப	டு
வே	த	ளி	ய	ப	ன	கு	தி	வே
டு	கா	வ	ம	து	ன	எ	கா	யோ
ன	ம	யே	சி	போ	வ	ழி	ல	உ
னி	த	ன	னை	இ	ய	ன	னை	ம
ண	ரு	ன	உ	றெ	செ	க	த	ண
ம	ப	த	நா	கி	து	க	க	கு
ன	வா	நி	ப	ரு	ண	எ	க	எ

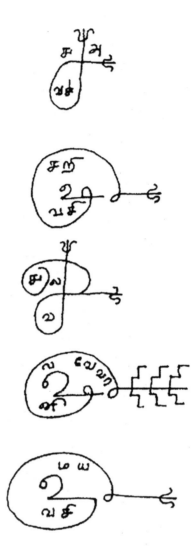

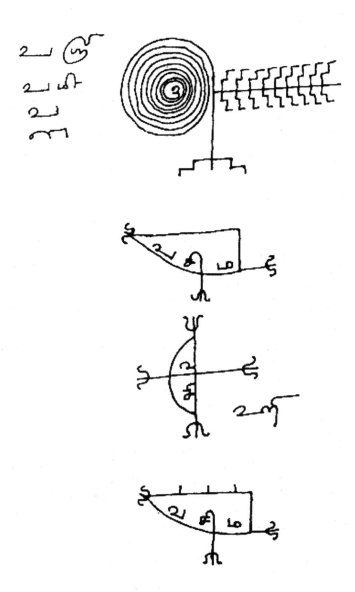

Next, dry roast Bauhinia recemosa, copper sulphate, cinnamon sticks, Peucedanum vulgaris, cardomomum, thyme seed, Aconitum, galangal, and Morinda tinctoria on hot coal on the bark of a plantain tree. Then add the juice of wild cilantro boiled in buffalo's urine, cactus stem, Calotropis bark, and Moringa indica bark that have been soaked in a female goat's urine for nine nights and ground together. Next add powdered snake skin, and put the decoction aside. Take equal quantities of cumin seed, poppy seed, onion seed, balloon vine root, yellow-berried nightshade root, and spiral ginger, powder them, add to this Mexican poppy seed and Indian coral tree seed, roast all this on a peacock tail, and grind. Smoke a monitor lizard out of the bush with frankincense, cut off its tongue, and mix it with the above-mentioned powders. Eat a bit of the mixture each day for 45 days after chanting "Ohm Baghadeva Bhavani Chamundi." The lips and tongue will turn black. The body will acquire the fragrance of white dead nettle. The eyes will cool down and the limbs will turn cold. Next, boil the bark of kulamban, pomegranate, Indian coral tree, theeneeli, thurunji, podanganari, and Cissus quadrangularis in a mixture of hen's blood and monkey's blood, and strain. Then take a wasp that has just built its nest and is about to go into hibernation, and add it to the mixture. Grind all this together, calcinate it in open sunlight, grind again, add the tongue of an albino crow, make balls of it, and eat a ball each day for 45 days.

Dead-Brain followed the instructions written on the old palm leaf Kulla Chithan had given him. And his body did change, his eyes did cool down, and his body did take the fragrance of white dead nettle. Now that he was equipped with the spell to charm women, he started to wink at every woman who happened to pass him. Unfortunately, before long, he happened to wink at a plainclothes policewoman and she threw him in the gallows and beat him up.

Dead-Brain, having thus been cheated by Kulla Chithan, next sought the help of an astrologer, who told him to write the words *Aryan Yoni* a hundred and eight times for a sure victory. Ninth-Century-A.D-Dead-Brain began to write.

Aryan Yoni Aryan Yoni Aryan Yoni Aryan Yoni
Aryan Yoni Aryan Yoni Aryan Yoni Aryan Yoni
Aryan Yoni Aryan Yoni Aryan Yoni Aryan Yoni
Aryan Yoni Aryan Yoni Aryan Yoni Aryan Yoni
Aryan Yoni Aryan Yoni Aryan Yoni Aryan Yoni
Aryan Yoni Aryan Yoni Aryan Yoni Aryan Yoni
Aryan Yoni Aryan Yoni Aryan Yoni Aryan Yoni
Aryan Yoni Aryan Yoni Aryan Yoni Aryan Yoni
Aryan Yoni Aryan Yoni Aryan Yoni Aryan Yoni
Aryan Yoni Aryan Yoni Aryan Yoni Aryan Yoni
Aryan Yoni Aryan Yoni Aryan Yoni Aryan Yoni
Aryan Yoni Aryan Yoni Aryan Yoni Aryan Yoni
Aryan Yoni Aryan Yoni Aryan Yoni Aryan Yoni
Aryan Yoni Aryan Yoni Aryan Yoni Aryan Yoni
Aryan Yoni Aryan Yoni Aryan Yoni Aryan Yoni
Aryan Yoni Aryan Yoni Aryan Yoni Aryan Yoni
Aryan Yoni Aryan Yoni Aryan Yoni Aryan Yoni
Aryan Yoni Aryan Yoni Aryan Yoni Aryan Yoni
Aryan Yoni Aryan Yoni Aryan Yoni Aryan Yoni
Aryan Yoni Aryan Yoni Aryan Yoni Aryan Yoni
Aryan Yoni Aryan Yoni Aryan Yoni Aryan Yoni
Aryan Yoni Aryan Yoni Aryan Yoni Aryan Yoni
Aryan Yoni Aryan Yoni Aryan Yoni Aryan Yoni
Aryan Yoni Aryan Yoni Aryan Yoni Aryan Yoni
Aryan Yoni Aryan Yoni Aryan Yoni Aryan Yoni
*Aryan Yoni Aryan Yoni Aryan Yoni Aryan Yoni**

---

* Those lady readers who took the time to count the above to check if the words have been correctly written a hundred and eight times may stop reading the book at this point and go do some useful work.

0°

CHAPTER 10

THEIR EYES WERE blindfolded. Candles were brought in, and used to burn off the hair from their heads and their groins. The entire camp stank of singed hair.

The flame licked their genitals, and they yelled in pain. Those who yelled loudest were scorched longer. They screamed as if the earth under them was quaking. Bits of burnt flesh dropped from their charred genitals. The stench of roasted flesh filled the air. Their howls were just long strings of vowels, with no recognizable words. Next they were burned on their chests, cheeks, necks, armpits, thighs, stomachs, the soles of their feet, their chins and buttocks. After the candle game came the chili powder, sprinkled from a plastic canister with nine holes. Then they were laid out on long benches, on their stomachs. Spoons were brought in and used to check if their buttocks were well-cooked. For those whose meat was not sufficiently well-done, Thayumanavan ordered that the candles be brought out again. Once the flesh was well-cooked, spoonfuls of it were fed to the other prisoners. Those that refused to eat it had hot metal rods rammed up their anuses.

Though the flesh had roasted and fallen off the bones in many places, he was still alive.

"Water, water," he pleaded.

"He wants water," said Thayumanavan, "attend to him."

They made him stand and tied him up again. A sepoy raised a ladle of hot oil up to his face. He who had begged for water now cried out loud, and clenched his teeth so hard he bit off his tongue. A hot metal rod was pressed to his cheek; unable to bear the pain, he opened his mouth wide to yell, and then they poured in the oil.

"Idiot! He asked for water, why did you give him oil?" demanded Thayumanavan.

"There's a water shortage in the country," replied the sepoy.

"Fine," said Thayumanavan, "but be careful. Don't let his cholesterol level shoot up."

The sepoys fell to the ground rolling with laughter. Some even had tears in their eyes.

"Comrades, where is your sense of humor?" asked Thayumanavan. "What are you, a bunch of machines?" He turned to a short, fat prisoner. "Aren't you supposed to be a writer? How can you claim to be a post-modernist if you don't understand satire? You're still stuck in the age of Greek tragedy.

"So make them laugh already!" he commanded the sepoys.

The prisoners were laid on the benches and bound. The sepoys brought in crabs and cockroaches and let them crawl about over their bodies.

After a while their knots were loosened. They were served shit on tin plates. "Eat with your hands," yelled Thayumanavan. "Have you ever seen pigs eat shit? The way they slurp it up, *saluck-paluck?* Eat it like that. Relish it!"

Some of them ate it, and threw up. Those who could not eat it, or who refused to eat it, were taken aside, and bound to benches again. On Thayumanavan's orders their front teeth were knocked out with a hammer.

A few had their molars extracted with pliers. Then they were untied. Some of them fainted from loss of blood. "Comrades," Thayumanavan said to those who were still screaming, "you need more tolerance. Now kneel on the floor." Poisonous caterpillars were strewn on the ground in front of them. "Eat," he commanded. Those who would not eat the caterpillars had their fingernails torn off.

Boars were brought in with their legs bound. Some of the prisoners were untied and ordered to fuck the pigs. Then they had to hug the pigs and sing:

Kannathil muththamittal—ullam than
Kalverri kolluthadee
Unnai thazhuvidalo—Kannamma
Unmaththu magudhadee

When I kiss your cheek
My heart brims with wine
When I hug you, Kannamma,
I am drunk on you

Thayumanavan separated those that could not sing in tune. "I've thought up some new games especially for you," he said. "Come along."

0°

Chapter 11

I THINK IT WOULD BE good for you to see a psychiatrist, said a Lady Reader.

Lady Reader, if there was a psychiatrist who could do me any good, then he would also be able to eradicate starvation, famine, corruption, exploitation, megalomania, and jealousy, he said, vexed.

Don't be angry. I'm only saying this because I care about you, said the Lady Reader.

It's not surprising, in any case. I could see it coming on for some time, said another Lady Reader.

This is what had happened: The Honorable Tamil Writer had stopped saying hello to Muniyandi.

I'm fed up with writing in Tamil. I want to write in whatever language I choose: French, Spanish, Swahili, Arabic, Hebrew, Yiddish, Masai, Zulu, Soddo, Luganda, Kimbindhu, Looba, Kigongo, Ngutha, Lingatha, Yombo…

You are unfit to even stand on this Tamil soil. You should be exiled.

Word'll kill. Word'll win.

Muniyandi, your word'll kill.

Word'll kill, yell, sell, kill, will, well

Pill, till, call, cull, pull, pill, mill, well, wheel

Vaal, vaal, vaal, vaal, vaal, vaal, vaal, vaal, vaal

Vaal, vaal, vaal, vaal, vaal, vaal, vaal, vaal, vaal

Nine swords were spiked into a huge lump of earth and bound with a wire at the hilts. Badrilal placed the lump on top of a pole, then placed the other end of the pole onto an upturned wrist, and lifted it high. As someone else pulled the wire away, Badrilal threw the pole and the lump of earth and the swords into the air, then immediately lay flat on the ground, as the nine swords showered down and stuck into the ground in a circle around him.

This was Muniyandi's favorite street circus act. But on that day a sword accidentally pierced Badrilal's chest. Since then, Muniyandi has avoided street circuses.

What was it that killed Muniyandi? Was it the word, or the sword, or Fate?

He has stated that it was words that killed him. But there are several other competing theories about how Muniyandi met his end. A Lady Reader claims that, after some stupid fight with The Honorable Tamil Writer, he ran away to Africa, swearing he would never set foot on Tamil soil again, and joined a drama troupe in Rwanda. She says he wrote letters to her continuously for eighteen months. What happened after that? There was no news from him for a while. Then, after another nine months, she received a letter from a girlfriend of his from Burundi. Read it for yourself, she said, and handed it to me.

What's this name, Lady Reader? It's weird-sounding.

The letter was surprisingly weird, too.

Muniyandi joined our drama troupe in 1989. There were nine of us, including him. Muniyandi learned our language easily. On account of the growing ethnic tensions, we were conducting street plays amongst the Tutsi and Hutu people. Sister, it now seems as though all that was useless. It's depressing to realize that nothing more can be done. We made our escape after hiding among the scattered dead for days. Countless rotting corpses, human bodies with the eyes dug out, the tongues chopped off, limbs amputated, riddled with bullets. Sister, I can't find any reason to go on living. I have lost all faith. Including Muniyandi, five of our troupe members were killed; only four are left now. Eighteen lakhs of us have crossed the borders into Tanzania, Zaire, or Burundi as refugees.

We learned so much from Muniyandi. He came from a land so far away and taught us about experimental theatrical forms, like **forum theatre** and **invisible theatre**, from regions afar.

He was an extremely funny man. He was the clown of our troupe. I would say the most important thing we learned from him was the concept of satyagraham—non-violent protest—although he didn't believe in it himself. I don't know much about your country; perhaps you dull people don't have enough revolutionary spirit to have any use for satyagraham, and perhaps Muniyandi's opinion made sense in that context. But I think it's a concept our people need.

Muni has told us a lot about your country. I heard that you get married to a person who you don't know, who you've never even met. Still, in spite of hearing so much about it, I can't think of your nation as much more than a shape on the map of the world. (Have you noticed that the shape of your country resembles the shape of our continent?) To really know a country, you must dive into it, drown in it. Like Muni dove in. But, unlucky soul, the spot he dove into was the mouth of a frothing volcano. When the eruption died down, Muni's flesh, bones and muscles, now charred and cooked, flowed down along with the lava. How can I search in the lava? Even as I write this, my eyes flood with tears. It's absurd, sister—he, born in a distant land, comes here to melt in the lava. I could find nothing of him in those ashes… I started off telling you about something different, and here

I am lamenting about his loss. Ah yes! The non-violence we learned from him. But he always spoke of sathyagraham with disgust. Maybe it did not suit your country...

Once I told him, **Muni, you are so docile.**

Yes, he agreed, **we have been trained to be docile by the Britons. We have been trained for the past hundred and eighty years.**

From this I can get some idea about you Indians. But I don't think the impact of nine hundred people shot down in a war is as great as a single woman fasting to death. I don't know, I could be wrong. I am no good at sociology or politics; I'm an actress, an actress with a toy gun inciting my audience to protest. It was Muniyandi who asked me, *Do you even know how to shoot a real gun?* I never expected to encounter guns. But I watched as countless bullets flew in front of my face; those bullets chewed through 5,40,000 lives.

That was all nine months ago. Sister, I got your address from Muniyandi's diary. I am not even sure this letter will reach you. I'm writing to you anyway. I'm fed up; I don't really care if it reaches you or not. Even now, when I think of the way Muniyandi used to clown, I laugh. He used to cook dog meat here. We would be scared and angry: *Isn't dog meat poisonous? Won't we die barking like dogs if we eat dog meat? There are so many here who have died barking like that!* But Muni used to joke that such a death would befall us only if the dog ate us, not if we ate the dog. (By the way: is it true that dog meat is the staple food in the country just next to yours?) He would butcher and skin the dog, clean its meat, and cook it too. Sometimes he would try to scare us with the skinned dog head. A skinned dog's head! He would perform a Yoruba dance while holding it. I took a photograph of him dancing. I still have that photo safe with me.

The first day he cooked dog curry, he ate it all himself. We wouldn't touch it. We waited for a few days, and after we were sure he wasn't going to start barking, we also tried it. Mmm, it was tasty! But Muni boasted that even if he were to cook a donkey, it would be tasty. He was very proud of his cooking. Okay, listen to this joke. On the first night that he ate dog curry in our camp—we were camping in Kibuÿe, a city I will never be able to forget until the day I die, the army massacred 1,80,000 there alone—while we were all asleep, we heard a dog barking in our room. We switched on the light to find Muniyandi barking, his eyes bright red, spittle foaming from his mouth. We all began shaking with fear. Miriam, a member of our troupe, even began to cry. Finally we found out he was just acting, deliberately trying to terrify us. He teased us for several days after that. That dog curry reminds me of so many things. Tell me—even though there are so many elephants in your country, you don't eat elephant meat. Why? We eat it. Muniyandi loved it, too. In fact, the very first day we met that big fatso, he asked us where he could get elephant curry. I believe a minister in your country once told a group of starving people to eat rats. Politicians are the same all over the world. But there is a difference in our country; here, politicians shoot the people down, barbecue them, and then eat them.

Okay, I'll stop here. Tonight the memories of Muniyandi and my other comrades are crowding my thoughts so much...

0°

CHAPTER 12

THE COUNTRY SAT in the center of Africa, a tiny circular dot on the map. Zaire to the west, Tanzania to the east, Burundi to the south. A population of 81 lakhs. No coastline, no trains, no industry. Rampant malaria and venereal disease. Languages included Swahili, Kinyarwanda, and several other dialects. High above sea level. Rocky soil. Bamboo forests with elephants, lions, and gorillas. In the north, the volcanic peaks of the Virunga Mountains, Mount Karisimbi the tallest of them at 14,787 feet. In the west, Lake Kivu. Eighty-one percent of the population belonged to the Hutu ethnic group, who were largely farmers; they were said to be the first settlers, though nobody was sure when they arrived. The Tutsi came after them, perhaps around 1350. They were cattle herders. Six feet nine inches tall, and strong. No other race in the world could match their strength. They were a warlike people, trained as soldiers. They may have come from Ethiopia; wherever they came from, once they arrived, they dominated the other ethnic groups. Although they were not great in number, they soon became masters over all the others, owning and controlling the land.

The aboriginal people of the land, the Twa, were pygmy hunters and potters. Their population numbered about 90,000.

The country was colonized first by the Germans, and then by the Belgians, but they were only rulers on paper. The real power rested with the Tutsi. For over 360 years the country was ruled by a Mwami, a feudal lord of the Tutsi tribe. In 1962, the Hutus rebelled. Power was snatched away from the Tutsi. Nine thousand of them were massacred. They fled to other countries as refugees. This was the same year in which the university in Butare was founded. But after a few years the Hutu president was assassinated by Tutsi soldiers—this is all stuff you can learn from old newspapers. You don't need me to tell you. But Nano, *how* the nine thousand Tutsi were massacred will not be found in our archives. Those details are locked in the collective memory vault of the Rwandan people.

But I happen to have come across that information. My Algerian girlfriend, Nafisa, translated an old Hutu man's notes, written in Kinyarwanda, about how he and the other Hutus massacred the Tutsi.

Our war has begun. It began a long time back. We finished off Rukansu Mwimba, Ntare Rutaganzwa Rugamba, Mwami Kigeri Rwabugiri, and all the other Tutsi Mwamis.

We swirled the Tutsi children in the air and smashed their heads onto the ground, into trees and rocks, and killed them. We chopped off the Tutsis' genitals and their tongues. We dug out their eyes with thorns. We threw them alive into the canals. We tore the children and babies in two. We built a stake nine feet tall and sharpened the top, made a Tutsi sit on it, and pulled him down by his legs. It was not easy to tear apart a Tutsi. The body would split in two up to the neck and stop there. After that we would cut up the Tutsi's body. We made some of them swallow red hot coals. If a Tutsi escaped, we would chop off his head; our children even today tell tales of watching headless bodies run for miles. We did all this in full view of the other Tutsi. The Tutsi should see this, the Tutsi should learn to fear us. We used to fear them; we did all this because of that fear—the fear of death. Do you know what another word for death is? Tutsi. We were teaching death what death was.

Did you hear what the old Hutu had to say, Nano? Now the Tutsi and Hutu are killing each other by turns. They don't impale people on stakes anymore; more often, they use tyres. You should see that, a man running with his arms pinned to his body by a flaming tyre! But whatever the old Hutu man said is nothing new to us. If you doubt me, just ask Thayumanavan. Right now, the same thing is happening again, in Ethiopia. The TPLF (Tigray People's Liberation Front) and the EPLF (Eritrean People's Liberation Front) are at war with each other. Eritrea is fighting to become an independent nation. But the recent famine has sent 1,80,000 as refugees to Sudan.

And so it keeps happening again and again. Not just here. Everywhere.

CHAPTER 13

THE FOLLOWING HEADLINE grabbed my attention as I was doing research in the archives of daily papers from years past: THE MONKEY THAT DEFILED A WOMAN. I looked up the meaning of monkey in the dictionary, and discovered that it was an animal. But I still could not understand the word *defile*. The state-approved lexicon did not include this word. When I looked it up in the dictionary of forbidden words, I saw that it meant *to sexually overpower*. Still, I couldn't make any sense of it. What was it to sexually overpower someone? Was that even possible? Why didn't she just suck out his blood?

The story is complete. All that's left is to title it. Since it falls under the genre of science fiction, I think this title will do. It's not fancy, but I think it will suit what follows.

THE WOMAN WHO DEFILED A MONKEY

Piyyo wrote that while researching old manuscripts in some archive or the other, he had discovered that it was on the very same day ninety years ago that the leader of the Tree Party had held a very significant historical nine-hour-long fast. Riyyo wrote back saying that he had decided not to come, because he was worried that the Soil Party, which boasted about having splintered off from the Tree Party, would announce the celebration of their ninetieth anniversary. When asked "Why the hell didn't you tell me this when you called last night?" the only reply was a kind of noise:

Pee...kee...kow...nyoing

Pee...pee...kirrr...pee...kirrr...

the bastard will fall sick excrete deteriorate further when will you die donkey you dirty bitch Mudevi unwashed Mudevi bitch in heat working through the day singing and dancing when he arrives he will start to dance and oh what a dance he'll put her on his head and twirl ecstatic demented frenzy they will melt into each other like sugarcubes what's this? Why did these lines intrude into the story, only to generate confusion? Forget it. My fingers itch to draw the sari, but I hesitate—I'm worried that Ninth-Century-A.D.-Dead-Brain will accuse me of copying Kurt Vonnegut. In his book, Vonnegut drew a sketch of the ladies' underwear of an earlier era. Now I will draw the sari:

Of course, the designs on the sari would be many and varied. I said, "If you were to wear this sari, then Riyyo would not keep staring at your waist." This is a Lady Reader's letter found in a newspaper ninety years back:

Dear Editor,

It is said that it is part of Tamil tradition to wear a sari. I don't understand this tradition. When we wear saris the menfolk stare un-blinkingly at our waists. If, to avoid this, we wrap ourselves with the pallu and tuck the end in, there is still a large part of the waist exposed. The only way out is to totally cover our body, like a television news-reader. But, if we try to board a bus like that, the sari end somehow escapes our grasp, and then it becomes a struggle retrieving it in the crowd. Also, wearing a sari necessitates choosing a matching under-skirt. Now in a salwar-kameez, we can avoid all these problems. All we need are panties. We don't need to worry about losing the end of the sari or the waist being visible. Therefore, please desist from publishing any more letters that lament over Tamil women forgetting their traditions and switching over to salwar-kameez. Of course you men, who wear your pants without underwear so you can come and grind against us on crowded buses, will find this difficult to understand.

Riyyo: **You have upset me by inviting me to Kiyyo's place tonight. I gave you company the whole day.** *Phir bhi...* **you called me... I can't sleep tonight...**

Kiyyo is engrossed in his research on ancestral man. Riyyo is doing the same thing. And so they are known as science fiction authors. Those who opposed them demanded: "These two, who are writing about ances-tral man—do they *live* as ancestral man did? And if not, why do they want to write about him? Their blood must be sucked out as a punish-ment!" But Kiyyo engineered their escape by means of a super-intelligent feat. Kiyyo said: "Ancestral man. Sign. Arrival. Style. Structuralism. Style. A sign is contained in a sign, not in a language. Language is contained in language, not in a sign. Language and sign are completely different. I was asked, 'What is a sign?' I said, 'Look for the sign in the sign.' They are still looking. And so Riyyo and I escaped."

0°

Chapter 14

She is reading about the history of Peru. Her bones tremble on reading of the massacre by Pizarro and his men of 9000 Inca warriors. The Spaniards then installed a puppet ruler, Tupac Huallpa, before marching on Cusco. They captured the capitol city on September 18, 1539, and looted the golden treasures of the Sun Temple.

In my next novel, the protagonist will not know how to think. Her name will be Echo. She will be an audio mirror. She will do nothing but repeat what you say. Your speech will be her speech. Your word will be her word. Your silence will be her silence. She will not remember any name or identity.

Thinking these thoughts, she switches on the radio.

The radio news says that 270 skeletons have been found in the hospital morgue in Sarajevo, that only 90 of them have so far been identified, that the task of recovering the 9000 bodies in Srebrenica is underway, and that the excavation is revealing more and more bodies.

She shuts off the radio and puts on Mozart's Requiem Mass.

0°

CHAPTER 15

THE DOG IS CHASING Muniyandi matter movement the animal's bark was as loud and menacing as the roar of a lion matter attempts to exist on its own the ground seemed to quake matter is engulfed by other matter he is running down Barakhamba Road in the dark cold lonely night running for his life matter will give its best effort to exist on its own matter tries to occupy the universe it has come too close about to start a spring that could span the world it is because man understands himself as human that he tries to study the universe the distance between himself and certain death was shortening matter has continuous movement within it death is now dependent on time and space it is only because the neutron understands itself as neutron that the big bang took place the dog is now a word existing on this page when meaning is sought after there are many other meanings that are lost here in this moment illusion from now on it makes no difference if the physical movement is real or a hallucination does Borges have this physical movement of matter in him death is certain now **language is a set of games** the fear of death lends him speed the scientific truth of matter in language is negated here I can feel the hot breath of the dog at my heels Robbes-Grillet looks at matter as nothing but that as his terror increases so does his speed but isn't this reminiscent of eighteenth-century naturalism the body burns like fire **Iannis Xenakis** is able to recreate the burning sun with his **electro-acoustic**

music breathing has now become a fiery storm is the seepage of light similar waves that measure the sky **density and sonority of sound is an eighty-thousandth of a second galaxy explodes traveling in mind and cosmos using group theory and mathematical logic into the concept of mathematical probability stochastic music theory is created** is it possible to become nothing with no space or time only a few moments separate me and death the athlete covers ninety meters in 9.81 seconds I stand on the precipice defying gravity **the density of nuclear matter is 45 trillion times more than that of osmium the densest element occurring in nature this has a parallel with Bernoulli's law of large numbers which states that as the number of trials of a random experiment increases the percentage difference between the expected and actual values goes to zero.**

I jump off the precipice and then catch hold of the edge flipping a coin nine hundred times increases the chance that the number of heads and tails will at some point become equal the dog follows the natural count is lucid and systematic his chest feels as if it will burst fish jaw blahblahblahblahblahblahblahblahblah waves scream to shatter the universe Henri Charrière calculated the patterns of the ocean waves and planned his escape accordingly can I escape Xenakis is an expert in physics but The Honorable Tamil Writer says *music is the sacred worship of creativity* that creativity will come alive as melody it will become visible to human eyes he runs forgetting time space self and the other the Yoruba dancers have reached the climax a sensation of melting into the atmosphere **okantomi okantomi okantomi okantomi okantomi okantomi okantomi okantomi okantomi** blahblahblahblahblahblahblahblahblah Guevara's face is visible amidst the swirling Yoruba dancers the sound recedes into silence **poses in different forms** lingam yoni yin yang **lines squares circles space music** *vilambit* structures symmetry time swastika dimensions universe light and attuned body movements frog crocodile tiger snake animalistic forms **such as a replacement of old and dilapidated wiring replacement of electrical fittings and fixtures and installing additional electrical points are badly required frequent** breakdown of electricity the working hours have been increased and there is almost darkness no toilet for the lady staff members or the male staff members whereas about four hundred and fifty members are working in this office psycho fever in the minds of the staff members because of the appearance of live snakes requested that availability of funds to the tune of nine lakhs two thousand three hundred and four (Rs. 2,50,659 for minor civil works plus Rs. 6,51,645 for electrical repairs) in '63 when pump-sets were introduced into rural areas it relieved the sexual frustrations of the rural youth all genitals have been confined in the darkness hidden from sunlight for centuries only humans copulate face-to-face Garcia Lorca tries to escape death in Madrid by fleeing to Granada, but is caught there and dragged through the streets we are reminded of his *House of Barnada Alba* and its women **embarrassing problem of premature ejaculation** suddenly remembering the similarity between running and punching he turned his thoughts to Yamaguchi the karate master spending hours practicing *sanchin* under a mountain waterfall *kiai* develops with kiai you can do impossible things **Seikenzuki** breaks a 180 kilogram block of ice with his bare hands **front forward push multiple stroboscopic photographs taken at intervals of 1/180th of a second show the fore-fist moving at the speed of nine meters per second she breaks wooden planks measuring 27 × 18 × 1.8 centimeters and concrete slabs 45 × 18 × 9 centimeters thick the physicist analyzes and evaluates the factors the elasticity of the materials the acoustic properties of the materials and the amount of energy each material accepted from the fist concrete's elasticity is such that if it bends a millimeter it will crack wood will fracture if made to bend 1.8 centimeters Michael Feld Professor of Physics at the Massachusetts Institute of Technology** Muniyandi thought about the distance between the object and the punching fist and its speed it is the same as the distance between me and the dog chasing me *Le Diatope* **is a composition of cosmic music combined with African drums Japanese** *tsuzumi* **noises made by rubbing stones on cardboard and music based on mathematical probability theory.**

0°

CHAPTER 16

I HAVE TO STOP MYSELF from building up these imaginary stories about Muniyandi.

First, his claim that The Honorable Tamil Writer was ignoring him, purportedly because he made derogatory statements about the Tamil language, is a lie. In fact, The Honorable Tamil Writer responded by challenging Muniyandi to a wrestling match.

Also, Muniyandi didn't really die in Rwanda. There is clear evidence that he came to Kashmir after the Rwandan Civil War. He wrote a letter to Surya from Kashmir. I even read it. It was damaged, though, and all I could make out were some recipes for Kashmiri cuisine. You don't believe me? Here, I'll quote from it.

Wazawan Researchers believe this dish originated in Central Asia. It takes nine hours to prepare and nine people to cook it. The cooks must rent huge cauldrons, which they bring on horse-driven carts. The cooking is done in the open air. The ingredients are:

[*This portion is missing, the paper having been eaten away by bookworms.*]

Aside from the many run-of-the-mill roadside dhabas, I have made a list of places to head for specialty items. The Friday night buffet at the International Centre—the chicken curry served at Sriram College of Commerce on Wednesday—the fabulous evening tea at St. Stephen's College in the university campus—the Sunday lunch spread at Hindu College, which could be compared to a wedding dinn…

[*The portion after this page is lost among Muniyandi's notes.*]

0°

Lal Salaam

A man who appears to be the chief security officer calls Muniyandi and Tamil Selvan over, and begins to speak.

THAYUMANAVAN: So, Comrade, tell me.

[TAMIL SELVAN *remains silent.*]

THAYUMANAVAN [*To* MUNIYANDI]: Look at that, sir! Even when I speak to him respectfully, he still remains silent. How can I get anywhere with this interrogation if he won't coöperate? Ahem. Well then—*you* tell me.

MUNIYANDI: Yes, yes. Ask whatever you want, and I shall answer you.

THAYUMANAVAN: There. See? An author is an author. But an activist can only be an activist. What kind of an activist are you? A wanker activist? Oh, Comrade, please don't be angry with me because I said "wanker". If you were in my shoes, you would talk the same way. I'm sick and tired of criminals. Sometimes I wish I could chuck this job and find work as a college lecturer somewhere. What was the use of spending my school days and college days learning all that philosophy, sociology, literature? It's my sad fate to have ended up here. Of course, our Comrade will take issue with that statement. He doesn't believe in Fate. But what about you, sir?

MUNIYANDI: I'm not sure if I believe in Fate or not.

THAYUMANAVAN: [*To a* CONSTABLE] Dey! Five-Naught-Four! We're going to have a debate here. Go bring us some tea. [*To* MUNIYANDI] He probably assumes this is some petty theft case, the idiot. Nobody here has any brains, sir—including me. I used to have some, but now they're gone. After all, I can't very well cast myself in the role of a dog, and then refuse to bark, can I?

Sir, please don't misunderstand me. Go ahead and write; who am I to advise you? I won't raise any objection. I've read your novel; I like your writing. I think your anger is justified. But I prefer the ironic passages to those that are just angry. Which passages do I mean? Oh, like this, for example: "The communists discovered collection boxes even before the world discovered tin." Wonderful irony, sir.

MUNIYANDI: But you shouldn't attribute that quote to me. That's a line from an anti-communist character in my novel.

THAYUMANAVAN: Oh, yes, you're pro-Left, aren't you? [*Turning to* TAMIL SELVAN] What do you say, Comrade? Have you read any of his writings?

TAMIL SELVAN: Yes, I have. They are clearly the result of the ruinous influence of American culture. His writings are an insult to my soil, my people, and my language. He has mortgaged his brains to the Euro-American dogs. He is a pervert who can write about nothing but sex. We, the People's Front, will punish the likes of him.

THAYUMANAVAN: So, you're a militant sympathizer, too. I thought you were just a communist. Good, good! Even I support the militants—only moral support, though. The same way I support homosexuality. I've read that even Socrates was a homo. [*To* MUNIYANDI] I have just a single word of advice, sir. Write in support of whatever you want: military revolution, countercultural revolution, homos—there are so many causes!—but you must restrict such anti-establishment writing to *English*. What's the point of writing in Tamil, and then ending up here? I feel bad for you.

Yes, I read your novel, and I also read Dead-Brain's review. Why did you have to respond to that? It's almost as if you've exposed yourself in public. You should be mature enough to accept it if someone calls your novel shit. A writer should have that much pride. People are idiots; of course they will say such things. It would have been surprising if they *hadn't*. It was only because you responded that the police department sat up and took notice. When you put everything out on the table like that, people start wondering whether it's literature or politics. Do you respond to everyone who calls you for a fight, sir?

Look at our Comrade. He's hardly even opened his mouth. There are no misunderstandings or philosophical debates between him and me; it's just straightforward war. He wants to destroy the state, so he bombs us—and sooner or later we police will finish him off in an encounter killing. Why do you have to come in the middle and confuse everything?

You want to know something? Your bank heist hero, Mayta—this Tamil Selvan here is his lieutenant. What do you say, Comrade? [TAMIL SELVAN *remains silent.*]

The great Tamil poet Thayumanavar said: *Kill the Word.* Our comrade follows that to the letter. I am a faker, not worthy of the name: you are the real Thayumanavan! Do you know how I got this name? My father was a Christian and my mother a Muslim. Theirs was a love marriage, even way back then. And this is how they named me. What communal harmony! I'm not saying this just because they were my parents. If everyone were like them, we wouldn't have all these riots. Ahem. Fine. This interrogation is concluded. Now for the national anthem! All things should be brought to a proper conclusion. Comrade, what's your opinion of the national anthem?

TAMIL SELVAN: It's the national anthem of India. We'll have nothing to do with it. We are creating our own anthem for our new nation.

THAYUMANAVAN: Fabulous! Dey! Five-Naught-Four! Are you listening to our Comrade here? You bunch of idiots! He's got more brains than all of us put together. A man should be like him. I'm jealous of you, Comrade. [*To* MUNIYANDI] You tell me, sir, what is your opinion of our national anthem?

MUNIYANDI: I look at it as a text, a literary text.

THAYUMANAVAN: Aha! What an answer! You should be awarded the Nobel Prize for this reply. I wonder how your brain thinks this way. I was also like that, many years back. Ahem. Let us complete the interrogation now. I'm tired too. Let's all rise and sing the national anthem and call it an end. Please rise.

> [TAMIL SELVAN *remains seated, while* THAYUMANA-VAN *and* MUNIYANDI *rise up to sing.*]

THAYUMANAVAN and MUNIYANDI: Jana gana mana athi-nayaka jayahe / Barata bagya vidhatha...

> [*The* CONSTABLE *tries to make Tamil Selvan rise forcibly, but to no avail.* MUNIYANDI *looks at Thayumanavan, who is singing at the top of his voice, gripped with patriotic fervor.*]

THAYUMANAVAN and MUNIYANDI: Punjaba, Sind, Gujarata, Marata / Dravida Uthkala Vanga...

> [*The* CONSTABLE *signs to Tamil Selvan to get up.*]

THAYUMANAVAN and MUNIYANDI: Vindhiya Himachala Ya-muna Ganga / Uthkala Jalasi Charanga...

> [*The frustrated* CONSTABLE *punches Tamil Selvan in the face.* MUNIYANDI, *scared, raises his voice to match Thayumanavan's.*]

THAYUMANAVAN and MUNIYANDI: Tava suba name jage / Tava suba ashisha mage / Kahe tava jaya gatha...

[TAMIL SELVAN *continues to sit. The* CONSTABLE *can only wring his hands and stare at him.*]

THAYUMANAVAN and MUNIYANDI: Jana gana mangala dhayaga jayehe / Barata bagya vidata / Jaya he / jaya he / jaya he / Jaya jaya jaya jaya he!

[*As they finish the anthem,* THAYUMANAVAN, *overcome by ecstatic passion, nearly collapses. He takes a moment to recover, and then turns to the constable.*]

THAYUMANAVAN: Dey! Idiot! What was that dance you were doing while I was singing the national anthem? Don't you know that you should stand at attention?

CONSTABLE: No sir, he was refusing to stand up, disrespecting the anthem. So I had to slap his face.

THAYUMANAVAN: You may be as old as a donkey. But you have no brains. Tamil Selvan is not a constable like you. He is a revolutionary! Please excuse us, Comrade. I will punish this idiot who insulted you. You want to know what the punishment is? [*To the* CONSTABLE] Dey, you! Fuck Tamil. Now. What a punishment! Horrible! It just came to me in a flash. Come on! Ready, start! Everybody wake up, let's give them a round of applause.

CONSTABLE [*Shouts*]: **OBEY THE ORDER!**

[*He kicks* TAMIL SELVAN *in the stomach.* TAMIL SELVAN *groans and doubles over. More men come forward to hold him down tight and rip off his pants. The constable strips naked and begins thrusting his organ into Tamil Selvan's ass.* MUNIYANDI, *scared out of his wits, starts to sweat profusely.*]

0°

HALVES

GENNY...

The term *homosexual* did not come into widespread use until the eighteenth century. Until then, as far as sex was concerned, both women and children were fair game. Sex was defined narrowly, as vaginal penetration, nothing more.

Long, long ago, humans did not look like we do now. They were huge creatures with two heads, four hands, four legs, two sets of genitals, four buttocks, and two noses. Since they were endowed with super strength, they paraded their arrogance before Zeus, and in turn he tore them each into two halves and knotted up the skin so that they would never be able to regain their previous strength. That knot is what you call the navel. So each severed half is constantly searching for its other half to become full again. It is only when I can relate to my half that my existence becomes complete. It was Nano who completed me, Patroclus who completed Achilles, Jonathan who completed David, and Bheeman who completed Duryodhanan.

0°

Chapter 17

He flipped disinterestedly through the newspaper. The previous day, eighteen bombs had gone off across the city within eighteen minutes... The state government reported eighteen people dead... The opposition claimed that the death toll was actually 108... The bombs were set off on a crowded city bus, in a hospital, in a school, at a place of religious worship, at a bus stand, at the railway station, at a vegetable market, at the police commissioner's office, in the town square... The Chief Minister blamed the attack on a foreign hand... The opposition leader blamed it on the ruling party's incompetence... Previously, when the opposition party was in power, and 333 bombs went off, they had fiercely debated the home ministry's report on the death toll of 666... "It is a crime to set off a bomb; it doesn't matter who sets it off. Even if it was God setting it off, it would be wrong," the tired film star said in an interview immediately after returning from a three-month holiday in San Francisco... To the question "Why is there so much sex and vulgarity in your movies?" the **RAW** actress replied, "What, do you think I was born with clothes on?"...

He shut the vernacular paper and picked up the English daily.

The insistence of the White House spokespeople that no matter how many women sucked the president's cock, or how many times he demanded that they suck his cock, it was wrong to expose these details in the media... the lack of accountability in America's orphanages... pro and con arguments for America's attack on Iraq... a massacre in Algeria... a report on an election propaganda poster that read "Do you really want to vote for a woman who owns 999 pairs of shoes and 9999 saris?"... a passionate op-ed piece from a Tamil poet asserting that the Tamilian breakfast was idly-dosai-vadai-uppuma-and-pongal, not bombs... an interview where an actress claimed that a scene from her forthcoming film, in which she stood astride two moving motorcycles while singing, was a cinematic first... a communist Chief Minister who had held on to the post for thirty-six years said he would resign to take the Prime Minister's post if offered... a long report from the opposition berating the ruling party for not being able to eradicate poverty even forty-five years after chasing out the British...

He put away the dailies.

0°

CHAPTER 18

SHE IS ALONE at home.

She reads Eve's Weekly.

She rises and stretches.

She gazes out the window.

There are new shoots on the mango tree branches.

He stares at her from the street corner.

She sees him, too.

What do you want, she says with a motion of the hand.

You, he says.

He flashes a secret smile.

Come up, she motions.

She disrobes.

She gets him naked.

She hands him the whip.

She lies on the bed on her stomach.

Lash, she says.

He hesitates.

Rising, she tastes his organ.

She bites gently.

He cries in pleasure and pain.

She drops it, and lies back on the bed.

Lash, she says.

He lashes.

Harder, she says.

She lifts up her buttocks.

The strokes fall and she groans with pleasure.

She lies on her back.

She lifts her breasts high to receive the lash.

She spreads her legs.

The bed is wet with her blood and her juice.

She licks up both.

She lays him on the bed.

She tastes his organ.

She rubs his cum over her face.

0°

SHE WAS THE BEAUTY of the town. She had brushed aside any number of young men bearing love letters and poems. He made *her* accept his love. Nobody understood what his trick was, but he made her want him. At some point, though, she doubted the depth of his love.

The next day, he branded his thigh with an iron rod. Later, she swept aside his veshti, caught a glimpse of the wound, and became distraught. He expressed his love for her in this and countless other ways, until finally he ran off without informing her.

There were crowds of girls streaming out the gates of Indraprastha College. The roads were empty except for these girls. He saw them from a distance, and unzipped his pants and took out his thing. When the girls caught sight of it, the thing reared its head. The girls ran away screaming in fear, *Oh Shit Oh Shit!* A few of them appealed to God, in English, for help.

He always keeps a tiny pencil stub in his pocket, and never misses a chance to scribble on a toilet wall. His favorite game is to sketch famous godmen and intellectuals in the company of cabaret dancers.

When venereal disease sores appeared on his lips, he whispered, "J.K., J.K.," and then went around kissing every woman he knew on the lips, to pass on the disease.

His favorite pastime was to send telegrams to people he knew informing them of deaths.

Whenever he saw someone being beaten up by a crowd on the street or on a bus, he would rush to join in and give his share of the beating until the poor man dropped dead. Sometimes he would also use his secret *varma* knowledge of pressure points.

While riding on the bus, he would take out his mysterious tool and rub it against the woman standing in front of him until he ejaculated his love juice all over her clothes. Once, he did this on a nun's white habit. She was too deep in contemplation of the spiritual world to notice, but the women around her, realizing the grievous insult to God and religion that had occurred in their presence, raised their voices and demanded to know which devil was responsible for the dirty deed. He pointed at an old man standing next to him, and quickly slipped out.

He thinks bharatanatyam should be performed in the nude.

He believes women should also be able to wear the sacred thread.

The following incident took place in the southernmost part of the state, during the tourist season. It was a bright moonlit night. He was walking alone on a road when he suddenly came upon a statue of a famous caste leader. He knew at once what he had to do. He went back to a cobbler he remembered seeing next to the bus station. The cobbler was lying asleep on the road, using his prosthetic limb as a pillow. Emboldened by the cobbler's loud snores, he stealthily opened the sack of chappals lying next to him. His mind was busy concocting excuses he might give if the cobbler woke up, but his heart was fearless, focused resolutely on the mission. He pulled out as many pairs of chappals as he could. On his way back to the statue, he also found a length of old nylon cord on the road. Once there, he tied the chappals together in a string, and, looking around carefully, garlanded the statue. Then, before the break of dawn, he jumped on a bus and fled from the area. The evening newspaper reported that eighteen people had been beheaded in the ensuing caste violence. The rioting had even spread into nearby towns. After the riot had raged for nine days, the police arrived, with shoot-at-sight orders, and killed twenty-seven people. The policemen—well-built men who had been staying in camps far away from their wives and fed on chicken and mutton, so it was no real surprise that they had indulged in homosexuality to relieve their tension—tried to catch the rioters, but they fled to the hills. So, instead, the police broke into their homes and sexually abused their women. (All this he learned only from the Tamil newspapers; the English dailies were preoccupied with the ethnic violence in Africa.) It was reported that thirty-six women were defiled. The police commissioner announced that all the suspected policemen would be immediately suspended. But eighteen of these policemen pleaded innocent before the Supreme Court, claiming that, since they did not possess the essential male organ (Chee! What kind of bullshit term is "male organ"?), there was no way they could have been responsible for the alleged defilement.

During his college days—even before that; during his school days—he would pick on pretty girls in his class, find out their addresses, and send them guy-girl, girl-girl, guy-guy, guy-girl-guy, girl-guy-girl, guy, guy, girl, girl—ooh la la, there's no end to this, let's try a different tack—some-times alone, sometimes with multiple partners, sometimes with animals, sometimes with objects—no, no, no, no, that isn't right either, let's get to the point—he would send them smut books in the mail. Of course, it goes without saying that he would never mention a name or return address, and would always write with his left hand. At times he would laugh to himself in class, looking at the girls whose faces were swollen from crying all night. When he got especially excited he would write love letters (again with the left hand), and sign with the name of some other boy. Many a girl was forced to discontinue her studies because of this. He had been the persistent, anonymous nightmare of several girls' fathers all through his schooling. When he continued this game in college, a girl named Shanthi sent a reply:

Dear Surya,

I saw your letter. Hmm... maybe not a letter, but a poem. A poem dripping with honey. But how daring of you to write to my house address! Imagine if my parents had seen it! Even the thought scares me. You shouldn't be such a daredevil. But I guess you're not really that daring—you sit at the desk right next to mine in class; why didn't you give it to me there? It's not like I'm going to eat you alive. Mmm... but I *would* so like to eat you. You have such cute chubby cheeks. I want to bite your cheeks and just sink my teeth into them, Surya. Imagine you coming to college the next day with my teeth marks on your cheek! Even as I'm writing this I can't stop laughing—I almost choked! Aiyyo... I'll write more later... Amma is coming...

Surya, Amma saw me choking while I was trying to write, and she brought me a glass of water. She also started scolding me, saying "Why don't you concentrate on what you are writing?" How do like that? Where was I... your cheeks. I want to bite your cheeks, your beautiful fingers, your earlobes... mmm... no, I won't tell you where else. You'd think badly of me. Wait until you see me.

The Thief of Your Heart,
Shanthi

P.S: You've described me so beautifully in your letter... Does that mean you're looking at me all the time instead of listening to the lectures?

P.P.S.: You've compared the shape of my back and my front to sand dunes! I'll never be able to write like you. You are a poet.

P.P.P.S: Please give me a reply to this when you see me.

He gave her his reply, went to the movies with her, twined his fingers with hers in the dark theatre, and kissed her hands. After several such efforts he thought he might even have a chance to screw her. She consented, on the condition that he use a rubber. He agreed but secretly pierced the tip of the rubber with a pin. After the act, however, he saw that the love juice had not been able to get through the tiny hole. From this he came to understand that the love juice was so thick it needed a larger hole, and so the next time, he made a small snip in the tip with a pair of scissors. He checked that through the slit he could see sun, tree, shrub, vine, goat, cow, sand, hill, man, woman, bus, house, direction, air, fire, taste. Once he was sure that the entire universe was visible through the slit, he wrapped it back up in the packet, and used it the next time he screwed her. Seeing that all the love juice had made it through the slit without her knowledge, and feeling pleased, he disposed of the rubber. She missed her next period, and became perplexed, but was too afraid to tell her mother. Nine weeks passed; she became really scared, and told him about it. "It can't be mine, darling. Have I ever come near you without a rubber? You know I haven't." Finally the mother came to know of her daughter's predicament and took her to the doctor. By then it was too late for an abortion. She came back crying to him, but this time he had another story.

"In a pond in a village, the men's section and the women's section were adjacent to each other. A man masturbated underwater and his viscous fluid of life swam across to the women's division and entered the womb of a chaste woman bathing there. When she realized that she had been robbed of her chastity and virginity and didn't even know which man had done it, she committed suicide. The village raised a temple in her honor; to build it, the ruler of the village had sack loads of sand from the deserts of Egypt and stones from Afghanistan carried in on the backs of the kings of those countries. For these acts, the ruler was awarded the titles of *The Lemurian Who Won the Soil of Egypt* and *The White Lion Who*

Won Over Afghanistan, honorifics which were carved into the stone of the temple.

"Apparently, this temple was raised before the continent of Lemuria was eroded by the sea, and oceanographers still believe they will find the remains of it if only they look deep enough in the Indian Ocean. And so, since I used a condom every time I slept with you, it must be that you got pregnant in some other way, like this chaste woman in the pond did."

He told her this, and left.

At the house of a prostitute, he lay on the floor and asked her to piss on his face. The terrified woman gave a loud scream and ran off. He stayed behind, of course, and demanded his money back; but instead he was beaten black and blue and sent on his way.

Muniyandi gave his friend Yagnavalkyan, who was a writer himself, a copy of the manuscript of his latest novel, a dialogue between fantasy and reality. Yagnavalkyan read through the novel, and that very night, he wrote his own novel, **Man Is Born Free**. Muniyandi retrieved his manuscript and gave it to the editor of a literary magazine for publication. "Of course, this deserves to be published," said the editor, "but the only way it can be done is to find a publishing house that doesn't have a single female employee." He went off searching for a publishing house without a single woman, but then Yagnavalkyan came to him and said, "Not to worry. I'll publish your stuff, with an afterword by George Bataille," and took the manuscript. In the meantime, the editor located a publishing house with no women employees and asked Muniyandi to hand over the notes for immediate publication. Muniyandi, who as a rule makes eighteen copies of all his manuscripts, gave him the copy he had in hand. When Mullusami a.k.a. Yagnavalkyan heard about this...

[*Muniyandi's notes after this are missing, the paper having been eaten away by bookworms.*]

It was after an unfortunate incident at a prostitute's house that Muniyandi started the habit of making eighteen copies of all his texts. When he was in her room, he asked her, as he usually did, what her name was, and continued on with "Do you like Pichamurthi?" At which she demanded, "We both know what you're really here for, why would you ask me a question like that?" To which, of course, he said, "Besides all that, I thought if you had read Pichamurthi, we could have a discussion about literature." The prostitute had immediately asked, suspiciously, "Are you a literary person?" To which Muniyandi smiled shyly and replied, "Yes." In a blink, the prostitute sat on the bed, raised her sari, and pissed all over the bag Muniyandi had placed there. For a moment Muniyandi just stood stunned. Then he yelled, "You bitch! What have you done? In that bag is my handwritten manuscript for a novel that will someday be translated into French and appreciated by the most intellectual minds of the world! You have destroyed that unique creation by pissing on it! Are you a paid coolie for the Marxists?" (After this, Muniyandi forgot his lines.) She yelled back, "Dey, you literary fellow, take your bag and scram, or I'll piss on you, too," and Muniyandi ran off with his piss-soaked handwritten manuscript, and after that he swore on the bag that forever onwards he would always make eighteen copies of everything he wrote.

In the days when Muniyandi was a part of the literati scene, a theatre troupe from Mexico visited Chennai and asked if it was possible to meet him; was he in the nation? To which Surya responded, what do you mean by nation? The Mexican troupe replied, if he were a writer in our country, he would either be living in exile, or he would be an ambassador.

Octavio Paz resigned his post as an ambassador in New Delhi in protest against the shootout during a student demonstration at a Mexican university twenty-seven years ago. **Elena Poniatowska** wrote about that incident in her novel *La noche de Tlatelolco*. The dictatorship came to an end.

Our authors have no identity of their own. They are either government clerks or the owners of petty shops, and write in their idle time at work. In a reader's forum of about 180, there are no women, not even writer's wives. So, judging by this standard, we figure Muniyandi too must be a clerk at the Mount Road Post Office, said Nano to the Mexican troupe.

It was only after hearing this that Muniyandi quit his job as a clerk and became a wanderer.

0°

Name: Deepthi. Wife of a friend. Works in a prestigious organization. Muniyandi often talks with her on the phone.

- That churidhar you wore the other day was gorgeous, Deepthi. It must have been designed exclusively for you by an expert tailor.

- No, I never lie. I'm speaking the truth.

- Don't tell me nobody's ever told you that before.

- I dreamt about you, Deepthi.

- No, I don't want to tell you the dream.

- Must I?

- We're on an uninhabited island. In a forest. Naked. We're plucking the fruits right off the trees. Bathing in the moonlight.

- What can I do? It's a dream, Deepthi, a dream. You asked me to tell you.

- Have you ever seen a blue film, Deepthi?

- What kind of bra do you wear? Traditional style, or modern?

- Did you know that Hitler's Swastika is a symbol of the sex act?

- What do you think of lesbians?

- How many sexual positions do you know?

- What's your favorite position?

- So because you are a woman, I'm not allowed to talk to you about this?

- **Hey why do you feel shy yaar.**

- Have you ever tasted semen?

- I'm crossing the line? Who decides where the line is, Deepthi?

oooooooooo

- You haven't spoken to me for nine days. I thought you were mad at me for crossing the line.

- What? Me? Angry? With you? How can anybody get angry with an angel?

- Yes, we should meet. Shall I come over?

- Fine, not your place. You tell me where.

- How can I say where? Wherever I am with you, that place will be heaven.

- Okay. Besant Nagar beach.

At Besant Nagar beach they made love, at the end of which he patiently strangled her.

Muttering "I have avenged George Bataille," he dragged her into the sea.

0°

Chapter 19

Muniyandi set out to write the greatest erotic novel in the world. For this he gathered telephone directories from every corner of the Earth: America, Britain, Spain, Scandinavia, Algeria, Azerbaijan, Serbia, Israel, New Zealand, Australia, Cambodia, Indonesia, China, Turkey, Egypt, Ghana, Zaire, Uganda, Costa Rica, and more. He has already spoken to 1800 women, and he's still talking. The expenses, of course, are sky-rocketing. The novel is shaping up to be the costliest production in the world. He is still receiving telephone directories from friends spread out across the globe. Every conversation he has with a woman, he records it immediately.

He believes that the **telephone directory is the most erotic book in the world**.

You can select any name you want from the list. You can tell that person all your fantasies. You can say all sorts of dirty words. There are some very exotic names in the X section. African names are sheer poetry: Xihale, Ngunji, Waringa, Kihahu, Kitutu... poetry, poetry. Through these pages of poetry, you must hunt for the names of women. Ambary in the Rio de Janeiro directory, Thuraya Maqbul from Tel Aviv...

"Maqbul, I am calling from India. I would like to fuck you," he said.

Can you guess what her answer was?

Never mind that. He called Clinton's private secretary and told her he would teach her every secret from the *Kokogam*; would she come? He called tired night-duty nurses and spoke to them for hours. Keeping time with an international clock, he woke up Celestina at dawn with a *buenos días*, and began to expound eloquently on the beauty of her breasts. He called up a woman named Kannagi and said, "You burned Madurai with your breast; these days they burn towns with bombs." When she asked who he was, he said, "Do not insult your creator; I am Ilango." She was confused, but he had her hooked. He went on and on.

At times, he had to listen to long strings of abuse. Sometimes he got very senior citizens on the line, and disconnected the calls. Those who somehow got his number called him back to berate him. Some women kept the connection live, without replying, and just listened to his hot load of words.

He has had many interesting experiences. Some women have fallen deeply in love with him and are dying to meet him. There are some husbands on the lookout for him too, ready to kill him. So he keeps his identity a secret; he is writing the novel in secret. In fact, in a recent letter to Nano, he writes that once the novel is finally published, he will have to go underground in order to escape from all these bloodthirsty husbands. He is also worried about the fatwas that Ninth-Century-A.D.-Dead-Brain, Mullusami a.k.a. Yagnavalkyan, and Ananthasami, the literary critic, are sure to pronounce on him. Muniyandi's friend Thirumalai told him that the entire Tamil literary world was eagerly waiting to see how Anathasami, with his strict moral code, would pan him.

In spite of all this, Muniyandi has not forgotten to acknowledge several people who helped in the writing of the novel. Friends who are employees of the Telephone Exchange, who cover his costs; friends who are rich enough to gather international telephone directories and mail them to him; there is a whole host of people who help.

Even as I write, Muniyandi is disporting himself with the women in his neighborhood, holding a cell phone in his left hand and a pair of binoculars in the right. He watches their activities through the binoculars, calls them up, and tells them he can see them.

- ○ Okay, where are you calling from?
- ○ I'm hiding behind the cement bench in front of your house and using my cell phone.

Before he can finish, she cuts the connection, steps out onto the balcony, and checks the cement bench. Nobody's there. He calls back immediately.

- ○ It's me, darling.
- ○ Is it really you?
- ○ Yes. Me.
- ○ Where are you calling from?
- ○ Definitely not from behind the cement bench.
- ○ I know that. There was nobody there.
- ○ When you cut the call, I guessed that you would come to the balcony. So I've moved to a new place now.

At this point, he cuts the connection. The next day he calls at the same time. She picks it up immediately, as if she's been waiting for the call.

- ○ So, you were waiting for me to call, eh?
- ○ Who are you? What do you want?

98

- I want you. I want your cunt.

- Please, be decent.

- Okay, decent. Fine. I need you. How's that? I need to taste your body. I want to carry you, I want to drink from you.

- I thought about you last night.

- I didn't think about you. At all.

- Mmm.

- Are you angry?

- Mm-mm.

- You have every right to be angry. You have every right to be anything at all with me, Monica.

- Mmm.

- What's got into you today? You're reminding me of a George Orwell character.

- I haven't read him.

- In his book he writes about a government. In that government is a Minister of Newspeak, whose job it is to limit the number of words people use. If there are too many words, people will use them to help them think. Too much thinking is dangerous for the state. So the Minister of Newspeak decides to allow people to use a total of only nine words. I think you should have been awarded that minister's post.

- I like to listen to you talk. You talk beautifully. I'll stay silent and just listen.

- I lied to you just now, when I said I didn't think about you at all. Take the number of hours in a day and multiply that by the number of seconds in each hour. I thought of you for that many seconds.

○ That's not good.

○ Why not?

○ You're a very great writer. I'm feeling guilty—you must have better things to do than to think about me all the time.

○ Isn't a writer allowed to have any love, or care, or affection?

ooooooooo

○ I was telling my friend about you.

○ What did you tell her?

○ I told her about what you've told me, in our conversations so far. She said *I* was lying, and you were telling the truth.

○ What's the truth, and what's the lie?

○ The truth is that you are always thinking about me. The lie is that I rarely think about you.

○ It's not enough to say I'm always thinking about you. You've become the very air I breathe. The beats of my heart, the blink of my eye, it's all become you.

○ You tell me all this, but you won't tell me your name.

○ Later.

○ Yesterday I was in the library going through all the poetry books trying to figure out who you were. But I couldn't.

○ I'm yet to publish my poems, Monica. [*Pause.*] Last night I heard the song **I Was Born to Love You**. I melted.

○ Stupid idiot.

○ Monica. Your name is as intoxicating as your voice. I want to listen to it forever. Your voice plays like a violin in my ears when I sleep. I try to imagine how beautiful the woman behind that voice must be.

○ Mm-mm. I'm not that beautiful.

○ Let's see.

○ When? Where?

○ I'm writing my telephone novel. I should be finished with it soon. We'll meet after that.

○ Oh yes, of course! But don't get a bad impression of me because I asked when and where.

○ Of course not. I know you, darling.

○ You are very romantic today.

○ I feel that way whenever I speak to you, Monica.

○ Don't try to pull that ajjal-gujjal with me.

○ I should tell you about a funny thing that happened a while back.

○ What?

○ I called your number expecting you to answer with an "Mmm". When I heard that, I started talking. But finally the person on the other end tells me she's your roommate.

○ Aiyyo! What did you tell her?

○ That your laughter last night was like scattering diamonds. I forgot to tell you that last night, so I had to say it. I told her about my dream of us on an unexplored mountain, bathing naked in a waterfall.

○ Aiyyo! Why'd you do that? Now she'll have endless questions…

oooooooo

○ I couldn't sleep last night.

○ Why, were you writing?

○ No, meditating. Horrible girl! The call got disconnected last night. I was unable to sleep without speaking to you.

○ I disconnected the call on purpose, you idiot! You didn't figure that out?

○ You did? My God! How could anyone in the world do such a thing? Don't you feel you've done something terrible?

○ Just wait. There are worse things in store for you.

○ What a witch you are!

○ You're no better. You said all kinds of awful things to my friend. Thank God she hasn't asked me anything about it yet.

○ Don't worry, she won't.

○ Why not?

○ I haven't said anything awful to her.

○ What? You didn't? But you said…

○ I lied. She did answer the call. But do you really think I could mistake her "Mmm" for yours?

○ Do you know what I would do to you if you were here right now?

○ What?

○ I'd beat you, pinch you, knock you on the head…

○ But darling, that's not punishment. Those would be wonderful gifts from my sweetheart.

○ Gifts, huh? We'll see what you think when you get them. So what else did you write? What have you been reading?

○ I haven't read anything for a few days.

○ Why not?

○ I'm too horny.

○ Oh come on. Life doesn't revolve around those few minutes. There's so much more to life than that.

○ What few minutes? I need a minimum of ninety minutes.

○ Does that include foreplay?

○ And after-play, too. No, I mean, not including any of that. Ninety minutes, minimum. A hundred eighty, maximum.

○ Oh God! Are you even human?

○ Nope. I'm a beast.

○ Come on, be serious, tell me the truth. Wouldn't you get bored? Is it some kind of piston, some machine you've got?

○ No. You're making the same mistake as all the other Indian middle-class women. That's why I've been thinking recently of giving up writing and becoming a sexologist. Nobody seems to fully understand the sheer number of different possible positions. First, her underneath and him on top, with her legs on his shoulders. A few minutes in that position. Just as she comes, he changes position. Now he lifts her up so that she's riding him. She comes again. He's still in control. Now they sit opposite each other. She's on his thighs. His thrusts are slamming into her inner walls, bang bang bang. She's tired. They rest a while and wash themselves off. The cool water shrinks his organ. Now she tastes it, moves it to the left and then the right of her mouth. *Don't bite too hard*, he begs, *don't bite too hard*. The organ rears up like a snake. She tries to take the full thing into her mouth. When it hits the bottom of her throat, she chokes for a second, takes it out of her mouth, and licks it all over. Then she takes just the head into her mouth and sucks it. Suddenly, when she's least expecting it, he flips her over to bury his face in between her thighs, thrusts his tongue into her secret place, rubs the long curve of her clitoris. Then he makes her kneel, takes her from behind. They go on like this, fucking, changing position constantly. Finally he gets on top of her to send his life juice inside her.

∘ Chee! You're horrible. She'd be completely tired and bored by the end of all that, don't you think? I think they should both take it slow and steady from the beginning and climax together. Then they should rest. That's the proper method. Like reading a good poem. Or like smelling a flower. Or like listening to **what can I do to make you love me what can I do to make you feel me**? Like listening to a saxophone. Like the first touch…

∘ If you say so, Monica. You may be right.

oooooooo

∘ Say something.

∘ What should I say?

∘ Anything.

∘ I don't feel like talking now.

∘ Why'd you call me then?

∘ I wanted to talk to you.

○   Then talk.

○   I forgot what I wanted to say the moment I heard your voice.

○   Tell me a dirty joke.

○   I can't think of any.

○   Think hard. I want to hear you tell me a dirty joke.

○   Maybe I'll think of some while we're talking. What are you studying now?

○   M. Com.

○   Do you talk about sex with your girlfriends?

○   Mm-mm.

○   Really?

○   Really.

○   ...

○   I don't think girls like to tell sex jokes.

○   I know lots of women who tell them. All kinds of hardcore jokes.

○   Really?

○   Yes. Can I tell you a joke now?

○   Mmm.

○   A poor farmer goes with a cow and a calf to sell. On his way he is waylaid by bandits who take his cow, strip him naked, tie him up to a tree and leave the calf behind. Nobody comes through the forest for a long time. Finally some villagers pass that way and find the man and untie him from the tree. At once he begins beating the calf. "Why are you beating that poor animal?" ask the villagers, to which he replies, "I kept telling this stupid calf again and again, 'I'm not your mother! I'm not your mother!' But it wouldn't listen to me!"

◦ ...

◦ How was the joke?

◦ Could that really have happened?

◦ What?

◦ What happens in the joke.

◦ Of course it could.

◦ Weird. Now I want you to whisper that joke in my ear.

◦ Even if I'm not next to you, I can give you an orgasm over the phone.

◦ How?

◦ What are you wearing right now?

◦ A midi skirt and a t-shirt.

◦ Have you ever masturbated?

◦ Chee! I don't even know what that means.

◦ Attained pleasure on your own.

◦ How can I do that?

◦ I'll give you a step-by-step. Who else is there at home now?

◦ Nobody. Nobody will be home for a while.

◦ Where are you in the house?

◦ In the living room.

- ○ Is the window open? Can anyone from the opposite house see you?

- ○ No, I shut it.

- ○ Take off your t-shirt.

- ○ Aiyyo! That's bad, isn't it?

- ○ Nothing wrong with it. Have you taken it off?

- ○ Mmm.

- ○ Unhook your bra.

- ○ Mmm.

- ○ Now stand in front of the mirror.

- ○ Mmm.

- ○ How is it?

- ○ I don't know what to say. Lovely!

- ○ Now take off your midi skirt.

- ○ Aiyyo, I don't know if I can do all this. It really seems bad. I'm scared. You say it's not wrong, but I think you're just saying that.

- ○ Look here, Priya. Why would I say anything to cheat you? If you don't want to do this, forget it.

- ○ Oh, please don't be mad. It's not that I don't want it. I'm just scared, that's all.

- ○ I tell you again, there's nothing wrong with it.

- ○ Fine. Tell me.

- ○ Now take off your skirt.

- ○ Mmm.

- ○ Now your panties.

- ○ Mmm.

- ○ Now look into the mirror.

- ○ Mmm.

- ○ How is it?

- ○ I didn't know I was this lovely, until today.

- ○ Now stick your left middle finger into your cunt. If that's uncomfortable, use your right middle finger.

- ○ Mmm.

- ○ Now move it faster. Up and down. Explore.

- ○ Mmm.

- ○ …

- ○ …

- ○ Hello.

- ○ Hello.

- ○ I thought you had disconnected the phone.

- ○ It was next to me. I couldn't do it with the phone in my hand.

- ○ I understand. You're panting. How was it?

- ○ I have no words to describe it. **This is the greatest pleasure I have ever had yaar.** But I feel as if I have committed a sin.

◦ There's nothing sinful about it. How can it be a sin if it gives you so much pleasure, and it doesn't affect anybody else? Okay. Go get dressed.

◦ I have to ask you something.

◦ Ask.

◦ Do other people do this, too?

◦ *Everybody* does this.

◦ I want to do it with you here next to me.

ooooooooo

◦ Hello, my dear Kavitha.

◦ Hi **dad**.

◦ Why are you suddenly calling me **dad**?

◦ Your voice is just like my father's. You remind me of him.

◦ Where is your father? What does he do?

◦ I haven't seen him for almost eighteen years. Except for pictures in the paper sometimes.

◦ What happened?

◦ When I was a child he was working in the movies. Suddenly he stopped coming home and moved in with a bit-part actress. He never returned to our house after that. He's a big film producer now. I went to his house to invite him for my wedding. But he didn't come.

◦ That's sad. What a huge sorrow to have in your life! I'm really surprised.

◦ Why surprised?

109

○ You always look so cheerful. You're always smiling.

oooooooooo

○ Oh, so you're still alive?

○ I guess so, my maker hasn't called me back yet.

○ It's a joke for you, is it? Where have you been all these days?

○ I'm sorry, Kavitha. I've been all wrapped up in my book.

○ I've been really wanting to talk to you.

○ Why? What's wrong?

○ I'm totally bored of my life. I was getting sick of waking up every morning and looking at the same old husband's face, going to work every morning, looking at the same old colleagues. I started wanting to die—just for a change of pace. That's when you started calling. Your voice is my only relief from my boring life. You are my dreams, my fantasies, my most mysterious secrets.

○ I don't know what to say, Kavitha.

○ You don't need to say anything. Just listen to me. I couldn't stop talking about you with my friend yesterday. She wanted to know what I thought all this was leading up to. I told her it helped remind me of my father. I didn't tell her that when my husband is on top of me, I fantasize about the figure of my father, and your voice.

○ …

○ Why are you silent?

○ I can't think of a reply right now. The words you just said are still ringing in my ears.

110

∘ I need to see you. I have to know how your face looks. I have to see your hands, your shoulders, your eyes, your fingers, your hair—the expression on your face when you speak to me.

∘ I'm just a voice, Kavitha. Just a voice.

0°

CHAPTER 20

Why aren't Tamil novels up to international standards?

How can those who store tiny pencil-sharpening penknives in their sword sheaths be expected to fence?

What is your response to the accusation that your novels are vulgar?

I've heard that an idiot, on seeing Michelangelo's artwork, once asked: "If he can draw so well, why couldn't he add some underwear? I can see the guy's ding-dong."

You have often said "I am neither a writer nor a poet." Why?

Initially I wanted to become a musician, a pianist. Even though I begged Neena several times, she ignored my requests, not realizing that the responsibility for creating a musical genius lay with her. Then, when I was eighteen, a customer of Neena's gave me a violin. That became the vehicle for my dreams. When Neena became too old for her business, her customers would spit on her face; some of the spit would spray onto me, as I sat outside the door fiddling away on my violin, until finally the violin disappeared and turned into a book. Next, I wanted to become a lepidopterist, but Nabokov had already done that. I had to choose something different. So I turned to ornithology. I have always loved birds.

If you were an ornithologist, why did you destroy birds?

My job is not about creation or destruction. When the incident to which you refer took place, I was in Harike. I was traveling across India doing research on birds. Because I was already an experienced trekker, I had an easy time of it. At Harike I recorded the calls of the Siberian **sandpiper**, the **linnet**, and the **bunting**. It was then that I was arrested. I don't see why the fact that I am an ornithologist should mean that I must also be a vegetarian! When I saw the **linnet**, my mouth started watering. I couldn't stop myself from shooting it down and frying it up with some chili powder. The **warbler**, the **European roller**, I ate them all. I was just as eager to taste them as I was to do research on them. Whenever I see a rare, exotic bird, I want to eat it. Apparently this is a crime for an ornithologist. Anyway, they arrested me.

Can you explain why the universe is actually nothingness?

This can only be properly understood if you have some time alone, with no interruptions from anyone else or any outside forces. First, become naked. You should not have any pornographic books or photos in your hands. Stroke gently for the first fifty-four minutes. When you feel you are about to ejaculate, stop. Let your mind wander. Your mind will start to race like a rabid dog's. Fantasize about all the women you know: your sister-in-law, your aunt, your best friend's daughter, the idol of a Goddess, that newsreader, that actress, your kindergarten teacher, the eighteen-year-old beggar woman on the road crying "Dear brothers and sisters, my father lost his legs in a train accident, he died when I was very young, my mother and my sisters and I are starving, dear brothers and sisters please help me", the soap vendor who sold you your new bar of soap, the servant maid, your women writer friends… At the end of all this, you will come to understand that the universe is actually nothing.

You once wrote a complete novel using only the words pain, body, thrill, flesh, blood, pus, serpent, *and* yoni, *and their synonyms. Deva Sharma, in his review, said he thought you needed a good painkiller.*

I'll give you a proper answer for this once I conclude my research on the relation between the nature of the universe and human life. I am beginning my research from Hanle, 189 kilometers southeast of Ladakh. My favorite comet is Hale-Bopp. During its recent close approach to the earth, I even forgot to eat.

Let's discuss your character Nano. Is she imaginary?

Nano mi vida. Nano mi niña. How many zeroes would you need to write down the total number of stars? Many comets are drawn towards the planets Saturn and Jupiter because of their gravity. There are always some shooting stars raining down on us. Some crash into mountain peaks, others escape the gravitational pull of the planet. After all, aren't the particles of comets converted into their shimmering tails? That's my Motherland, my Mother Tongue.

Why are you so angry with the vagina? In all your writing, you seem to beat it up black and blue; why?

If you want to understand my life, do not look at my writing. To understand my writing, forget my life. My life is separate and my writing is separate.

You think I am angry with the vagina? **I think the most beautiful delightful and wonderful thing in this world is CUNT it is egg it is aleph it is eye it is divine it is abyss = bottomless chasm deep gorge immeasurable depth abyss of despair primal chaos hiatus it is the abyss of my soul it is my magic land.** In that magic land I have fought midgets. I have brought them down with my cabalistic discs.

How can anyone possibly hate pussies? Black pussies, white pussies, brown pussies—I worship pussies. I kiss them. Pussies are very tasty.

0°

CHAPTER 21

A LADY READER, having read the novel up to this point, asked, "Just where is this story is headed? A proper story needs characters, and character development!"

"But who will create them? I live in a godless world. I live in a world full of injustice. I don't know what joy is, I don't know what sorrow is. I don't know who *I* am. Surya used to tell me about how his baby chicks would get carried away by kites. He would protect the eggs for twenty-seven days, help the chicks crack open their shells and come out, keep them warm, teach them to eat grain—all this just for a kite to come swooping down from the sky and carry them off in its talons. Not even nine chicks escaped. Tell me, where is the justice in this world?

"A tortoise lays ninety eggs. Even before all the eggs can hatch and the baby tortoises can make their way back to the sea, most of them are taken by sea birds. Only eighteen of the ninety make it back to the sea safely.

"When a female cricket makes her *chitek chitek* noise, the male cricket comes flying in to have sex with her, after which it drops dead.

"Ponder for a moment on the plight of this male cricket. Does he know that the female is going to call *chitek chitek*? Once he hears the sound, does he have any choice but to fly to her? It is his nature to answer her call, to have sex with her, and then to die.

"Where is the justice in this world? Where is the order? How can I create characters under such circumstances? If I can't even create characters, how can I possibly tell a story?"

"You can," said the Lady Reader.

"How?" asked Nano.

"I won't tell you. Find out for yourself," said the Lady Reader, and left.

0°

CHAPTER 22

SHE WAS READING the story of Null.

The symbol of Null.

Not only that.

What does it mean if a man shows his index finger and a curled thumb to a woman?

Yoni.

How can this symbol represent both Nullity and Creation?

Aren't Nullity and Creation different from each other?

0°

CHAPTER 23

DEAR SURYA,

There is no hesitation to express anger, hatred, ridicule or hysteria, but when it comes to openly expressing love, timidity takes over. Perhaps love is the biggest silence. The setting of my novel is man's battle against nothingness and conquest of the Word. But you have read it linearly, as you would read your life. Perhaps my story lacks the intensity of your criticism. I do not have a copy of the text to reread it again. I thought the nine words of your review letter were more beautiful than my novel, so why bother? Finally I realized that **I am a woman of understatements**, that there is nobody to listen to our whining and complaining, and that an **undertone** of self-criticism and self-mockery are enough. That realization made the presence of the story more meaningful. In truth, only when the notes for my novel lose their importance will our own lives improve.

With love,

Nano

0°

Chapter 24

THE RIVER FLOWS. On the banks are the smoking embers of the corpse burnt the previous night. A lone crow caws, bobbing its head. A path winds through the black babul trees. A serpent, shedding its skin like a magician, slithers into its burrow.

Gathering courage from the solitude, brimming with sensuality, she strips herself naked and dives into the cool water. She swims away from the banks, and then her head surfaces with a splash. She dissolves effortlessly into a mermaid with a swishing tail. She sweeps the water with her arms, swimming against the current back to the bank. When she gets there, dripping wet, the corpse reaches lustily out for her. Nano disappears into the shadows among the words in the stack of books.

0°

CHAPTER 25

STARS MORE THAN about 1.35 times the mass of the sun will be compressed to neutron stars of radius about 27 kilometers. It is possible to have stars with even greater masses, and therefore even greater compression, so that gravity will squeeze the matter out of existence to form black holes.

0°

CHAPTER 26

OMEGA CHANGES INTO alpha or beta or gamma or whatever the last letter is what is the end what is doing the writing **algunos aspectos del cuento** Muniyandi's omega is followed by Nano, Nano's omega is followed by Aadhi, Aadhi's omega is followed by Chromo...

0°

CHAPTER 27

SURYA TOLD HIS TRAMP FRIEND who aspired to become a nomadic artist like Henry Miller: "There's no need to worry. The state has taken over the responsibility of making you, and several crores of others, into Henry Millers. If you really want to become this country's Henry Miller, you should go out right away and buy yourself a helicopter or a horse. It would be even better if you learned to play piano, too." After that, Surya tried his best to steer clear of beggars. In spite of his best efforts, as long as he stayed in the suburbs, he was unable to avoid them. Surya was terrified of the electric train, the new symbol of the pathetic middle class. Even the tracks terrified him. On a drizzly evening, a middle-aged man had been crossing the tracks when he was attacked by a cobra; trying to escape, he ran onto the next track and was crushed under a speeding express train.

Yaman, the Lord of Death, who had come to Thirunelveli for the wedding of a dear friend, was surprised to see a mouse at the entrance to the wedding hall. "How is it that this mouse is here, at this place, at this time?" he muttered to himself as he entered the hall. The mouse noticed Yaman looking and whispering something to himself, and figured he would do well to get out of there before Yaman came back. He called out to an eagle that was flying overhead: "Sir, if you would be so kind as to do me a great favor, can you carry me away somewhere far from here?" The eagle answered, "I am on my way to Thongumalai, near Javvaadhumalai. Can I drop you off there?" The mouse, who didn't care where he went as long as it was far away from Yaman, agreed at once. As promised, the eagle dropped the mouse off at Thongumalai.

Back in Thirunelveli, as Yaman came out of the wedding hall, he noticed the mouse was gone. Then he, too, went to Thongumalai. There he saw the mouse happily nibbling away. He went up to him and told him, "Good thing you reached here before me. It has been fated that you should die now, here, at this time, and that was why I was surprised to find you in Thirunelveli. Now my job is easier." Saying this, he took his paasakayiru, the rope that frees the soul from earthly desires, and threw it around the mouse's neck.

The moral of this story is:

Fuck Yaman. Fuck you. Fuck the universe. Fuck the big bang explosion. Fuck everything.

At the train station, he saw several different sorts of beggars: the blind man singing devotional songs for the omnipresent lord; the guy singing old film songs, playing a harmonium strung around his neck; the woman with a newborn in her arms. In addition to these, there was a youth exhorting the public to "Protest! Boycott the election!"; a preacher warning of the Second Coming; a woman with a basket of saththukudi yelling out "Nine fruits for nine rupees" over and over again; a little boy with tiny lime-size apples, which he was trying to pass off as Kashmir apples; a blind vendor selling everything from nail cutters, covers for ration cards, identity cards, electricity cards, milk cards, season train tickets, ear buds, and toothpicks; a thin man with a nail as long as a knitting needle pierced through his tongue, his body streaked with turmeric and ash, the words *Om Muruga* printed on a yellow cloth around his waist, spittle dripping from his hanging tongue. Surya skirted around the man's begging bowl and walked on. Outside the station were a group of blind singers with a harmonium, accordion, dholak, and a small megaphone, singing songs from a thirty-six-year-old Tamil film. *The music directors of those days must have had these blind beggars in mind when they composed their songs. It may be impossible to avoid all this outside the station, but at least the preachers, beggars and vendors inside the train might be avoided,* Surya thought, and began traveling by first class.

0°

CHAPTER 28

AFTER MUNIYANDI had spent some time in Rwanda collecting notes for his novel *The History of the World*, his girlfriend carefully gathered them together, along with his newspaper clippings, and mailed them to me. At first, I wasn't sure what to make of the huge sackload of papers; slowly I started selecting things that I thought seemed important. As I went through them, it began to look as though Muniyandi was vacillating between documenting culture and counterculture. He would justify the massacre of eighteen lakh Cambodians by the Khmer Rouge, and then start writing about fossils of *Homo habilis* found in Tanzanian rocks.

Among the mountain of notes I found the following passage:

> Ninth-Century-A.D.-Dead-Brain and The Honorable Tamil Writer have prattled on and on about recording the history of their Tamil forefathers, about going back in search of their roots. Don't they realize that such a search would require them to go back eighteen lakh years? I can just as well claim that my forefathers were from Tanzania, since that is where the earliest human fossils have been found, and where man began evolving. So, you ask, is that why I came to Africa, to search for my roots? No, because if I shift my time machine into a higher gear, I can travel back many more lakhs of years and visit the very first form of life. Ninth-Century-A.D.-Dead-Brain

and The Honorable Tamil Writer, who claim to write about their soil, should first educate themselves on the origin of the soil itself. Let them listen to the tale told by the Martian meteorite that crash-landed in the snowy Antarctic wastes.

0°

CHAPTER 29

- WHAT WAS THIS SPACE, before this universe came to be, after the Big Bang?

- Is there a beginning or end to this space?

- What is limitlessness?

- What is time?

- When is timelessness possible?

- If this is how evolution happened, what evolved before evolution itself?

- Are our imaginations broad enough, temporally and spatially, to understand the origin of life?

- What comes after the end?

- Is it a lack of words?

- Is it a lack of knowledge?

- Why should I write in Tamil?

- Where did Tamil come from?

- If Brahmi, Greek, Devanagari, and Tamil letters all derive from that undeciphered script which originated in the Indus Valley civilization 5454 years ago, why shouldn't I take that unknown language as my Mother Tongue?

- Is The Honorable Tamil Writer aware of how many ethnic dialects must have been vanquished for Tamil to emerge as the language it is today?

0°

CHAPTER 30

Muniyandi went to a man with a fortune-telling parrot. "Muniyandi is the name, draw a card for the name, Muniyandi is the name," the man chanted to his parrot, "draw a card for the name, for Brother Muniyandi is it a good time, for Brother Muniyandi is it a bad time?" The parrot hopped slowly out of its cage towards the cards, and began to pick them off the top of the stack with its beak. When it picked up the ninth card, it threw it towards the men, and hopped back into its cage. The card bore the picture of a maid fanning a king, with the maid shown more prominently than the king. Only when he looked at the maid more carefully did Muniyandi realize it was not even a woman. *"Eunuch, eunuch! Brihanalai, Brihanalai!"* the parrot cawed. Muniyandi ran away from the place as fast as he could, wondering if his fortune would ever change.

He came to a stop at the Mount Road Post Office. In front of the building was a huge cut-out poster of a film star wearing a tiny skirt that left her practically naked. Below her, the male star was looking up at her. A few representatives of the Tamil Society were also standing there at the bottom of the poster, watching and waiting for the skirt to flutter in the breeze.

It was in 1980 that rural and suburban theatres began to openly screen blue films. For the typical Tamil husband, who had never even seen his own wife fully naked, the blue films were manna from heaven.

Muniyandi wasn't aware of this phenomenon. He had grown up watching *record dance* and listening to comedy dialogue cassettes, blasted through the village loudspeaker at functions celebrating a girl's coming-of-age, or whatever.

Characters: A woman selling vadai and a traveling blacksmith who mends broken vessels. The vessel the woman uses to fry vadai has a hole in it, so she comes to the blacksmith to repair it.

HE: What is this? Your vessel has such a huge hole!

SHE: What, don't you have what it takes to fill the hole?

HE: Why not? What I've got will fill this hole, and even a bigger hole. Show me, I'll fill it right now.

Wanting to see the film, Muniyandi went into the theatre hall. The newsreel was playing. The Chief Minister was formally opening a rehabilitation centre for the disabled. He went on to inaugurate more relief centers, for beggars, lepers, and orphans, and then to increase the compensation amount for women raped in police stations from 1008 rupees to 1188 rupees.

0°

AARTHI'S STORY

∘ SURYA, EVER SINCE I read *Existentialism and Fancy Banyan* I've been wondering where that Aarthi woman is.

∘ Lady Reader, I have no idea where Aarthi is. It's been years since I've seen her, I don't even remember how many. I haven't seen my Amma either. I've been keeping distance from everybody.

∘ Why haven't you seen anybody?

∘ I don't like the way they're behaving.

∘ Why should you care? Let them behave the way they want to, that's their nature. Why should you change for their sake? Don't you know the story about the scorpion and the ascetic? It is the scorpion's nature to sting, but the ascetic's nature to love all living things. So, even though the scorpion kept stinging him, the ascetic still saved it from the water and took it to the riverbank.

∘ Lady Reader, everybody knows that story already. Here, I'll tell you a story that nobody's heard before. Asuvam, the horse, was standing on a riverbank wanting to cross to the other side, so he stepped into the water, when Virchigam, the scorpion, also wanting to get across, but not knowing how, called out to him, "Asuvam, Asuvam, I want to cross the river, can you take me on your back?"; and so Asuvam placed poor Virchigam on his back and began swimming, at which Virchigam asked, surprised, "Asuvam, Asuvam, how is it that you can swim so well?"; to which Asuvam replied, "It is my nature to swim," at which point Virchigam stuck his stinger into Asuvam's neck; and as the venom traveled to his head and he began to drown, Asuvam cried out, "Virchigam, you idiot, why did you have to sting me now? Both you and I are going to drown!"; to which Virchigam replied, "Because it is my nature to sting," and then they drowned together and died.

○   Dey! Idiot, never mind about your nature, you need to be smart, too.

○   If I have to meet Aarthi, I have to meet Amma too. I haven't seen her for years.

So, at the urging of the Lady Reader, Surya began searching for his mother. Finally he discovered that she had been living on the next street all along, and went to visit her. But even she did not know where Aarthi was. He did, however, learn something from her about Aarthi's life story.

Aarthi, her husband Kamalanathan, and his mother, Kamatchi, were living in a tiny village near Madurai. They got no support from Kamalanathan's father, Rajangam, who had gone off to Chennai with a dream of getting Kamalanathan a chance as a playback singer for the movies. Meanwhile, young Kamalanathan slowly graduated from committing a few petty thefts for cinema tickets to working as a full-blown professional pickpocket.

He loved Aarthi very dearly, but she did not understand his love. She hated him, and she hated Kamatchi even more. Her fights with her mother-in-law would end with them grappling in the streets. That's when Kamalanathan would step in.

And what shape he would be in when he arrived! These days there's no need for policemen. The general public has taken over the role of enforcing the law. If they caught him picking a pocket, the people would band together and beat him to pulp.

Imagine how he felt, after a public beating like this, returning home to find Aarthi and Kamatchi at each other's throats in the streets. He picked up a piece of firewood and gave Aarthi a whacking.

"Get lost, pickpocket," she said, and actually hit him back.

"How dare you disrespect him!" said Kamatchi, taking the firewood from Kamalanathan and contributing her share of clobbering.

As Aarthi's head cracked open and began bleeding, Kamatchi suddenly switched over to her side. "After all, you are my younger sister's daughter. Why should you have to suffer for marrying a pickpocket?" she wept aloud, holding Aarthi in her arms.

While there are many people who have made it big picking pockets, it must be said that Kamalanathan did not excel at his chosen profession. He was often caught by the police (which wasn't so bad) or by the bus passengers (which was hell).

But there was no other source of income. Aarthi had become pregnant. Kamalanathan had a beautiful voice, but was yet to get a chance in the movies. How could he have, in such a godforsaken place? He would have had to make the trek to Madras himself, and make rounds at the studios, begging for a break. Trying to use his talents here would be like practicing horse-riding inside a mud pot.

Get lost, you dog. Go, like that fellow Rajangam and those other fools did.

They had a point. There was no news yet from Rajangam. And Kamalanathan couldn't just keep picking pockets his whole life.

Back when Pappamma was alive there was no problem getting enough food—at least, whenever she wasn't in jail. But when prohibition was lifted, her business collapsed. Whether it was due to that, or simply to old age, Pappamma fell ill. She, who had been at the top of the game, earning money like a man, running liquor bottles and casually walking in and out of prison, was now beached like a whale. She fell bedridden and never got up again. Even then, she laughed about it. "I am a Taurus. We never lie down, and if we do, then we don't get back up." It was true; she died without ever getting up again.

After Pappamma died, Kamatchi, too, fell ill.

In that village there was absolutely no way to earn any money. Even to find work as domestic help, you had to go to the city.

On the rare occasions that Kamalanathan made any money, he would be very loving to Aarthi. He would buy her flowers, take her to the movies. But even then, the day would end with him giving her a sound beating.

When she was full-term pregnant, they had their last fight. He called her a thevidiya. Her reply froze his blood.

"Yes. Of course I'm a thevidiya. I'm a whore. Even this child in my womb wasn't fathered by you. I swear on God's name."

Kamalanathan did not beat Aarthi that night. He couldn't even protest; without money he was powerless. He realized *that* was the source of all his problems. So the next day, he decided to pull a big job. He snatched a moneybag from a man coming out of the bank, and ran for it. But the bad luck that had followed him everywhere didn't let him off that day either. He was caught. He was lucky to survive the thrashing he got at the hands of the crowd; his life was saved by the police, who rounded the corner in a jeep just in time to rescue him. He *still* believed that it would be easy to strike it rich, someday; all he needed was a little bit of luck. Who would have guessed that he would get caught? That road was almost always deserted. It was high noon; the trees were motionless in the heat. It was just his rotten luck that a raucous funeral procession had to come by right then. The procession poured into the street just as he grabbed the man's moneybag and turned to run. The drummers and dancers pounded him into the ground. He still couldn't believe that he hadn't heard their loud drunken racket. He was convinced that the only reason he had survived to land here, behind bars, was that he was destined to *someday* make it rich.

The fetus was rolling around in the womb. It was difficult to sit, so she stood; as soon as she stood, she wanted to lie down. If she turned to her left, the fetus rolled to the right; if she turned to the right, it rolled to the left. It swam up and down searching for the exit. She sat up, tired, but could not stay in that position for long. She couldn't remember when the pain began. It started at the base of her spine and slowly spread until it seemed to engulf her entire body. Thank God for the old woman in the next hut; without her she and the child would have been dead and gone long ago. But where was that ayah now? Maybe the old hag too had pushed off to Madras, looking for a chance in the films. There was always a demand for mother characters.

And so here she was, alone, with a child ready to come out of the womb. She had believed Kamalanathan when he said he would care for her till the end; she had rejected the love of her mother, her father, her brothers and sisters for him; it had been eighteen months since she eloped with him, and now the man she had trusted was in prison.

She felt wetness between her thighs. Was it urine? No, her water had broken! She slowly moved to the front door. She tried to call out to the old woman, but her voice caught in her throat. It was an effort even to open her mouth. She bit into her finger, trying to overcome the pain. Her heart screamed "Ayah!", but the word refused to come.

"Don't worry, I am here," said the old woman, rushing in. A godsend! "Don't expect a miracle like this more than once! The next time you're stranded alone about to have a baby, I tell you, not even God can save you," said the ayah.

Aarthi looked at her with tears rolling down her cheeks and then turned to the baby. A boy child, cast in Kamalanathan's mould.

Memories of Surya crowded her mind. *How much he loved me!*

- Once you feel strong again, go back to your mother. That will be best for you.

- My mother went without food for days so she could feed me. But I ran away. Will she take me back, Ayah?

- Of course she will. I promise you. If you stay here there's no telling what might happen.

- I stamped on my mother's heart when I ran off with that cur. What face should I wear when I return?

- It's not like that. When your husband comes out of prison he'll drive you to your death. He'll take your son and turn him into a pickpocket too.

From the moment the baby was born, the old woman never left the hut. She made hot water and kanji, bathed the baby, didn't even go to work. Her profession was begging in the Madurai bus station.

Who is this ayah, Aarthi wondered, *who begs in order to feed me and my baby? My God!*

- Get ready now. I'll give you money for your bus ticket. I'm sure your mother will accept you.

- I don't want to leave you, Ayah. Once I get my strength back, if worse comes to worst, I'll sell my body to feed you and the baby. Please don't ask me to go.

136

o If you stay here, your life will be ruined. Go now.

Will I ever see this ayah again, before I die? Oh God, why should I alone be in this sorry state? She hugged the old woman and wept her eyes out.

She reached her home town. How long since she'd seen it! The eighteen months seemed like eighteen years. The first thing she noticed was Thennavan Tea Stall. Thennavan had been a classmate of Surya's. He had visited their home several times. Where was Surya now? Where else? Delhi, of course. She still hadn't even met her *anni,* her sister-in-law—a woman who had been married earlier, had a child, gotten divorced, and was now married to Surya. Surya might even have a child of his own by now. She would ask Amma about it, first thing—that is, if she was allowed to enter the house. Why was she thinking about Surya so much?

Her throat was dry; she wanted some tea. She untied the knot in her pallu and checked. She had a little change, but not enough courage to face anyone she knew yet. So she hastened home. As she passed the Perumal Temple, old Chinnachi recognized her, and began weeping: "Aiyyo, what's become of you?"

From Chinnachi, Aarthi learned that just after she eloped, her parents moved to Thirumalairayan Pattinam.

Her stomach rumbled. Somehow she managed to reach the bus stand again. The baby cried for milk. She sat in a corner and fed him. How could there be so much milk in her breasts, when her stomach was so empty?

She still had enough coins in her hand to reach Thirumalairayan Pattinam. It was a good thing she had not spent them on tea. By the time she arrived there and found the house, she was almost blind with hunger.

Finding a woman lying unconscious at her doorstep holding a newborn baby, Parvathi sprinkled some water on her face—and only then looked closely at her. Oh, what sin had she committed to have to witness her darling daughter in such a state?

Parvathi pushed away the past, and turned to the care and feeding of Aarthi and the baby. "Your body is tender now. You must eat healthy—for the baby, too," she told Aarthi.

A few days later, Kamatchi and Kamalanathan showed up. Parvathi, of course, didn't allow them in. So they stood on the street, yelling, demanding that Aarthi hand over the baby.

As the two sisters began to fight over the rights to the grand-child, Aarthi tried to push her mother aside and join the fight herself. Kamalanathan grabbed her by the hair and kicked her. Unable to bear watching her daughter thus abused, Parvathi ran into the house, came out with an arivaalmanai and aimed the blade at Kamalanathan's throat. Kamatchi saw her, and dragged Kamalanathan out of the way just in time, so that Parvathi lost her balance and fell.

Kamatchi and Kamalanathan stood in the middle of the street, threw handfuls of dust at the house, and cursed them:

"May you be ruined! May your daughter become the whore of this town! May your womb rot, and may your daughter's womb rot as well! May the pox take your children! May your family be wiped off the face of the Earth!"

After this tirade, Kamatchi dragged her son away. But it didn't end there. A call came for Aarthi and her parents from the police inspector. At the station there were long fiery debates, but the verdict was in favor of Parvathi. Maybe it was because Kamalanathan was unemployed, or maybe because Krishnasami, Aarthi's father, was a well-respected retired school teacher. Whatever the reason, it was decided that the baby would remain with the mother. Kamatchi threw some more curses at them in front of the police station, and finally went off with her son.

"Whatever has happened, has happened. At least from now on, you must be smart and careful," Parvathi warned Aarthi.

But Fate had different plans in store. Aarthi's life was to change course once again; this time the agents of change were a series of love letters from Saanthakumar, the neighbor.

Aarthi, you are the springtime of my life. I love you, read the first letter.

My life has no space left for love, read Aarthi's reply.

I love you more than my own life. If you reject me, I will have nothing left to live for, he wrote.

The tears in my body have dried. I have no more tears, no more love, to give you.

I need your love, darling.

I hate you. I hate all men.

But as the days passed, her coldness slowly thawed. She understood that his love was completely true.

He was an amazing lover, and he was ready to give up his life for her. "So what if you have a child. Didn't your brother Surya marry a woman who already had a child, and love that child as his own? The same way, I'll love your child as though he were mine," he said. He was a man of peaceful disposition, like Surya. His nature was true to his name: Saanthakumar, *prince of peace.* She called him Saanthan.

Aarthi learned that men could still be men without being rough. A man should have a touch of the feminine in him; it made him more complete.

Not long after Aarthi finally discovered her true and complete man, the news spread through the neighborhood. Saanthan's family, too, heard the news.

But Saanthan's parents did not share their son's peaceful nature. They became enraged. They were from a higher caste, and rich as well, which made them much more powerful than Aarthi's family. They placed a heavy padlock on Aarthi's front door, and demanded that the entire family vacate the town immediately. The men came with huge clubs in their hands, the women with filthy curses on their lips. Aarthi's father Krishnasami stood helplessly outside the house in his torn veshti and banyan. "I need to go to Karaikal, to bring Leela's husband. Please," he begged, "let me go inside to get a shirt."

"A shirt? You stood there like a towelboy while your own daughter was fucking her cousin brother, and now you want a shirt? Better you should be stripped of your veshti and underwear and forced to parade around town naked! This is all your fault. What right do you have to call yourself a father when your daughter is the town slut?" With that, Saanthan's father clipped Krishnasami sharply on the nape of his neck.

Krishnasami had a weak body and was not expecting this attack; he stumbled to the ground. Parvathi wept aloud, flailing her breasts and her mouth.

"What's the point of wailing now? Your daughter had a bad itch and started walking the streets. You should have scalded her thighs in the beginning. If you'd done that, maybe she wouldn't have slept with her own cousin and borne him a child. She wouldn't be checking out every man around, trying to snare them. Now she's just a bitch in heat," yelled Saanthan's mother.

Realizing that it would be dangerous to stay any longer, Krishnasami left for Karaikal, wearing the same torn banyan, taking along his wife, his daughter, and her child.

Through all this commotion Saanthakumar did not so much as peek out of his house. It was said that he was kept locked inside.

140

Krishnasami's sister Leela was married to a man from the fisherman caste. He held a government post and wielded a good deal of power in the community. When he saw the state in which his brother-in-law and his family arrived at his house, he immediately called for his men. The entire fisherman ghetto gathered there.

When the angry crowd descended on Saanthakumar's town, his household became terrified. There was a peace conference. It was decided that Krishnasami's family would move out.

Thus an event that might have sparked a major caste war fizzled out without making a mark on history.

Leela's husband found them a house in the same street. Krishanasami attempted to hang himself in shame, but of course, he failed in that too.

Parvathi was forever in tears.

Aarthi, after watching all these events, finally ran off, leaving her child behind.

"How did she find the heart to leave?" sighed the mother.

- So where is that boy? He must be about nine now?
- He's in an orphanage in Trichy. He got in on your uncle's recommendation.

He had a frail body, and the same sorrow-steeped eyes that seem to be found exclusively in orphanage children.

- What's your name?
- Surya.
- Your sister named him after you. She hasn't forgotten any of us. Her love is very deep.

- ◦ Do you know me?

- ◦ Mmm.

- ◦ During final exams last April, he came down with typhoid. He sat for the exams anyway. The orphanage ayahs took care of him. God knows what kind of care those coolies gave him. He returned after the exams looking like a bag of skin and bones. He was terribly worried that he would fail his exams. We can't keep him here; your father's pension money can barely feed us.

The young boy was stuffing his clothes into a ripped plastic bag, getting ready to leave.

- ◦ Will you go alone?

- ◦ Mmm.

Surya took some money out of his pocket, regretting that he didn't have much there, and gave it to the boy. He put his arm around his shoulders. "Study well, Surya."

Parvathi said she had no idea where Aarthi was now, but that she got letters from her once in a while. Beyond that, she could give no more information. On a hunch, Surya went to Trichy. There he learned more; that Aarthi had come straight to Trichy from Karaikal. She had used her body to earn money. She used to show photos of her whole family to all her customers: "This is my naina; this is my amma; this is my anna, Surya; this is aunt's husband, my mama—a very powerful man." Somehow, this had reached her uncle, who sent rowdies to chase her out of Trichy.

That's all I could find out, dear Lady Reader. Nobody knows where she is now. I cry her name to myself: Aarthi, Aarthi, Aarthi, Aarthi, Aarthi, Aarthi, Aarthi, Aarthi, Aarthi. I was no help for her. How her heart must be grieving, as so many strangers lay their bodies on top of hers. Even as I write this, I am shedding tears, cries Surya, a.k.a. Muniyandi, a.k.a. Nano, a.k.a. Misra, a.k.a. Charu Nivedita, a.k.a. Lady Reader, a.k.a.

That this woman's life, filled with pain, shame, hunger, betrayal, love, and loneliness, has now been reduced to mere words on a page, fills the heart with emptiness.

Her water broke at noon. She left to the hospital at once. They gave her an injection to hasten the delivery and put her on drips. She was scanned. They checked the child's position in the womb. She felt that the fetus had moved sideways. She tried forcing it out. She was still conscious. The child was born when the clock above her head showed 9:00. But her life was sinking away. She had lost too much blood. Her pressure was dropping. She could hear hushed voices all around her bed. The chief doctor wrung his hands. Her limbs shivered. Somehow, they brought her back on the road to recovery. There were many sutures. It hurt so much she almost bit the doctor's hand. None of the tranquilizers had any effect. He kept suturing her till midnight; she was screaming loud enough to shake the foundations of the hospital.

0°

CHAPTER 31

I'VE READ ABOUT YOU in Muniyandi's writings. Now I finally get a chance to speak to you. Yes, I've read every word Muniyandi has ever written. I'm sure there's no other lady reader who understands all the secret meanings behind his words, the meanings that he himself is unaware of. He's had several phone conversations with me, never realizing who I am. Do you know why he keeps on referring to the "Lady Reader" in his writings, again and again, helplessly? **His whole obsession is me.** Yes, that Lady Reader is *me*. That's my real name, Vasuki—*lady reader*. In his work, he has changed my name from Vasuki to Aarthi. I am his sister. It's because he feels guilty about what has happened to me that he keeps on agonizing about Greek tragedies, international politics, beedi-rolling child laborers, nuclear physics, history, Rwanda, women laborers working in stone quarries, ornithology, the Karmenian genocide, and prostitutes. He sees the violence suffused in all these things, and assuages his guilt with the thought that the violence in his sister's life is just a part of this larger violence. Poor soul. Violence is just a word for him.

As I have known him well for many years, I have come to understand that Muniyandi's life is different from his words. He is a coward. He has a silly, ongoing fear that his writings will become hugely controversial and be banned by the state. In fact, he's afraid of all sorts of things:

bus conductors, policemen, women writers, the literati, dogs, cats, mice, cockroaches, frogs, caterpillars, beggars, train tracks, and vehicles. He has confessed to me, over the phone, that once, when he didn't have exact change for a bus ticket, and the conductor reacted as though it were a criminal offense, he walked everywhere on foot for several days afterwards. Likewise with auto-rickshaw drivers. On that day when he wanted to go from Chinmaya Nagar to K.K. Nagar, an auto driver demanded forty-five rupees. He argued that the fare should be only eighteen, and finally bargained it down to twenty-seven. But the auto driver, piqued, drove so rashly, and took the bends in the roads at such dangerously high speeds, that when he finally got out of the auto he had a slight chest pain, for which he went to the doctor, who said that his blood pressure was high, and that he should stay in bed after nine o'clock, and should be careful not to lose his temper, and should not stay up too late reading, and several other *do nots*. After that, he developed a fear of auto drivers as well.

He often says that bus conductors and auto drivers terrify him even more than policemen. He is scared of all human company and wishes he could retreat to some lonely place. He drives me mad with his worrying: about whether his writing is anti-establishment, whether he'll be arrested for it, whether he'll be thrown in prison, whether he'll be allowed to write in prison, and if so, whether I will come and give him paper and pen. He apparently read a news item somewhere that quoted a few belletristic police officers who wanted him behind bars. He even started going to meditation classes, fearing that without them he would die of loneliness in prison. He asked me once if I thought meditation would help him control his mind and not lose it completely. How can such a coward write anything that will be a threat to the state? How can he write anything that will be a threat to social morality? In truth, all the social mores that he claims his writing is transgressing are the very standards by which he lives his own life. He's just saying these things to get noticed. But whether you are rejecting the social mores or accepting them, you are putting them in the foreground. Doesn't he realize that this counterculture he's talking about has been completely co-opted by the establishment? I think the greatest favor these counterculture writers can do us is to stop writing about prosititutes.

0°

THE MARRIED LIFE
OF NALINI AND SURYA

BEDSHEETS

○ Why are these bedsheets still soaking? Why haven't you washed them yet?

○ You didn't tell me you were soaking them. How was I supposed to know?

○ I asked you why they're not washed. Don't get smart. I don't need to tell you before I soak them.

○ I can't wash them now. I'm going out.

○ You know the bedsheets will get ruined if they soak for so long. If you'd bought them with your own money, you wouldn't treat them so carelessly.

○ If I didn't buy them, where did they come from? Did your cheap father give them with the dowry?

○ Don't blame my father for your worthlessness.

- I'm worthless, am I? It's your family that's worthless. They have looted the entire town's wealth and made themselves rich. Your father and mother have sold their consciences long ago.

- Your family is no better. Your sister ran off with her own brother. Your younger brother is licking his wife's foot. And you have the guts to talk about my family?

- If you can talk, why can't I? You're a shameless woman, just like your mother. You live here as my wife but you go around sleeping with every other man in town!

- Now that you know I'm shameless, get out of this house! If you have any sense of shame yourself, get out and never come back again!

TO BURY OUR FATHERS

- Where, pray tell, have you hidden away that novel?

- And which novel, exactly, are you accusing me of hiding?

- *To Bury Our Fathers.*

- What? But that novel is mine; what possible reason could I have for hiding it away?

- I strongly suspect that you hid it in order to get some sort of revenge on me.

- And do you really suppose I have no better method of exacting revenge? You actually imagine that I would be petty enough to try to punish you by *hiding a book*?

o   I searched the house high and low, but it was nowhere to be found. I have not an iota of doubt that you are the responsible party.

o   I had asked you translate it for me. Why would I choose to hide it from you now?

o   There's no way for me to know the answer to that. All I know is that I most certainly put it down right here, and that it is most definitely no longer in the same place. Aside from you, there is nobody else around to move it. A simple deduction follows.

o   You may say what you want about me, but please do not cast aspersions on my love for literature. I had that book mailed to me from a foreign country, and gave it to you to translate. I ask again, why would I want to hide it?

o   So be it; I accept that you have not hidden it. You have simply stolen it. Give it back to me, or there will be consequences.

o   How can I give you something which is not in my possession? You are just trying to find new ways to torture me.

o   I won't hear another word from you! You've sunk to the level of a common thief. I won't have you in this house any longer. Begone, this instant!

o   I won't! I will move only when I find a new house!

o   It makes no difference to me if you ever find a new house. You have to get out of here at once! Or else!

ELECTRIC CREMATORIUM

o   Gimme four thousand five hundred rupees.

○ For what?

○ What if you drop dead all of a sudden? Who's gonna get rid of your stinkin' corpse? I'm gonna hafta cover all those costs. Why should I pay out my own pocket?

○ What? Why should I drop dead all of a sudden? Hey, why're you worryin' about my body when I'm dead anyway, you fuckin' bitch?

○ Hey listen up, you better keep all this fuckin' bitch crap for some other fuckin' bitch. I refuse to spend my own money for your funeral.

○ Get your hairy-ass pussy outta here. If you don't wanna spend money on me then call the city corporation to come and take me away in a garbage truck.

○ Fat chance gettin' *me* to deal with all that crap. *You* call up the electric crematorium, ask 'em how much they charge, and then gimme the goddamn money!

○ You father-fucker! Why should *I* call and ask? Why should I give a shit about it anyway—I'll be dead, right? The dogs and foxes can eat my body, for all I fuckin' care!

○ Who are you calling father-fucker, you bastard? You want a slap across the face with my slipper?

ooooooooo

○ Did you ask yet?

○ About what?

○ About the electric crematorium.

○ Bitch! Why should I, you fuckin' whore? Why should I?

○   Who you callin' a whore, dickless? Your mother's a whore, and you're a whore's son. Get the fuck outta my house, you dog! You rabid mongrel stray! Get outta this house this second! Out!

0°

CHAPTER 32

AFTER SURYA SEPARATED from Nalini, he wrote a novel entitled *Revolver Rita*, in which he ripped her to shreds. A few womens' groups that read the novel demanded that he be expelled from the country. It was around this time that he met Avanthika.

0°

AVANTHIKA'S STORY:
An Abridged Version
of Avanthika's 324-Page Letter to Surya

DEAR SURYA,

Why I'm writing this letter—why I chose to write it to *you*—I'm really not sure. It's just that from the moment I saw you, I felt that you would be a good friend to me.

I wonder what you felt when you first saw *me*. Perhaps you thought to yourself, "Here is a woman with no worries, free as a wild sparrow." But in fact, my life has been full of pain and sorrow. Were it not for my daughter, Nithya, I would have ended it long ago.

There were nine of us siblings in all. I was the fifth. We were seven girls and two boys, of whom three died, and only six survived. So then I had a brother, two elder sisters, and two younger sisters.

My father worked at TVS. My mother was the principal of a school, but after the birth of my elder sister, she began to suffer from mental illness. There were three years between me and my elder sister. By the time I was born, my mother's condition had gone from bad to worse.

People tell me I was brought up by a dog. It was the house pet. If I wet the bed when I was a baby, the dog would bark to call my sister. If nobody responded it would drag my bed, with me on it, out to the others. It was like a circus dog—it performed all sorts of tricks in order to care for me. In addition to the dog, my neighbors, too, helped with my upbringing.

I used to be a cute, chubby baby. Maybe that was why the neighbors came forward to care for me. Even now they call me *Azhagi*. I will tell you later how my good looks became my enemy.

I never felt a mother's affection. We grew up without knowing the warmth of a mother's breast. My eldest sister Mythili, my akka, nine years older than me, was like a mother to me instead. Appa always preferred my sisters Geetha and Vatsala.

I still remember how Geetha used to always hit me and shout at me. I don't know why. I was in first standard then. Once we went on a school excursion to Mahabalipuram. Geetha told me not to come, but I was our class teacher's pet, and she insisted. Throughout the trip Geetha found reasons to hit me.

At the Mahabalipuram beach, Geetha surprised me from out of nowhere and pushed me into the surf. No one knew what to do. The waves were dragging me out to sea. Fortunately, I got stuck between some submerged rocks. I was rescued by a few fishermen. But by then I had swallowed a great deal of water. They told me that a fisherman had to take me by feet and twirl me around in the air to make me bring up the water. When I returned home, I told Akka what had happened, and she told Appa. But all Appa said was, "Who cares if the sea had taken her!"

I couldn't understand Appa, nor did I want to. Amma was getting worse. My younger sister Vatsala was a weak child, who did not learn to talk until she was three. Mythili Akka had to care for her too, which meant there was that much less love and affection for me.

I was in fifth standard then. Early one morning, there was a huge commotion in the house. I didn't understand what was going on. I usually slept with Akka. When I woke up, Akka was no longer by my side. I started to weep, and Geetha and Appa slapped me for crying.

I learned that Mythili Akka had disappeared, never to return. Appa's neglect and Geetha's oppression were sure to increase. Already we were depending on the neighbors for our food. God knows how we made it through school. After Akka ran away, there was nobody left for me. Amma's condition was worsening. If we even tried to go near her, she would chase us away. The neighbors began to treat us like beggars. If we went to their homes during meal time, they would drive us out. One day Vatsala and I went and cried to Amma that we were hungry. "Wait," she said, "I'll get you something to eat." She went into the kitchen and returned with an arivaalmanai. Vatsala ran off, but I got caught. When I tried to escape, she caught hold of my long plait, pulled me towards her, and aimed the blade at my neck. Luckily I ducked at the right moment; she was left with just the plait in her hand, and I fled.

After Akka left, I slept alone. I used to cry for her. I used to have nightmares about Amma cutting off my head, or being drowned by monstrous waves, or being beaten by Appa, and I would jump awake with a start. Not just in my dreams: even in everyday life, from the moment I woke up until I went to sleep I was either beaten or berated. *I'm sure you'll run off with someone. You're a slut. You're a whore.* And on and on. How can a father say such things to a young girl? It was only because I kept my inner child alive that I am able to survive in spite of this horrendous past. In my heart, I am still the girl in fifth standard, just abandoned by my Akka.

Around this time, Appa showed my horoscope to an astrologer who declared that I was the reason the family was going through such a bad time. It's difficult to write about what followed.

Even under ordinary circumstances I was afraid of my father. He treated me worse than a slave. Geetha's position had also become much stronger at home. Anna would take me with him everywhere he went, but once, he left me in Geetha's care. She was playing with her friend, who wanted me to join too. Do you know what Geetha did to me? She dragged me to a metal dumpster and dashed my head against it. My forehead split open and I bled. She just went on playing with her friend. Luckily, the family doctor was passing by and saw me, took me to his house, treated me, and kept me there till Anna came back.

I loved poetry, painting, and singing. I even got a chance to sing on the radio. Geetha gave me a thrashing for that. My sisters and I went to the same school. They would often play truant, but *I* would be reprimanded for it. I was a very timid girl. Only when I was in eighth standard did I come to know that Mythili Akka had gotten married to a man, and that now she had died. Perhaps because I resembled her, Appa hated me all the more. In spite of all this, I stood first in my class in both studies and sports.

Thinking of sports brings up other memories. Especially Vasumathi, my neighbor. We resembled each other a lot. I will never forget the days I spent with her.

Those were the days when we roamed free like birds. Krishna Nagar was a three kilometer walk down a mud path from the main road between Pallavaram and Pamal.

There were not many houses there in those days. The area was covered with fertile fields and orchards. At six in the evening, the jackals would begin their howls.

One evening, we played late, until after it had become very dark. On the way back home, we were chased by two jackals. Not knowing what to do, Geetha, Anna, Vasumathi and I ran into the Pillayar temple and hid behind the idol. Vasumathi's father came after a very long time and took us back home.

There are no fields, orchards, or streams left in that place anymore. The whole area has been leveled and built up. It is surprising how industrially developed it has become today, in such a short span of time.

The time I spent playing with Vasumathi was my only solace from the abuse I had to face at home. We would make tiny vessels out of wet mud, dry them, and then cook in them. I remember one evening when Vasumathi took some sugar, rice and dhal from her house without her mother's knowledge. Do you know how old I was then? Just ten or eleven.

We would walk from Krishna Nagar to our school along a mud track. There was a madwoman, Kaathaayi, who lived there. I wonder why it is that only humans go mad. Or do animals go mad too? You tell me, Surya. My mother, my friend Vasumathi—yes, she, too, went mad; I'll tell you about that a little later—those two boys in her married home... I, too, would have joined the list of lunatics, but for the mercy of God, who sent you to me.

I wondered who gave Kaathaayi her name. Where were they now? Did she have any relatives at all? Why did she roam around naked? Whenever someone called out her name, she would look around; I still remember the fear in her eyes. If a boy aimed a stone at her—because she was naked—that was it! She would make strange growling noises and come charging up to hit him.

Vasumathi and I, along with seven of our friends, used to fly around on our bicycles. We would play hide-and-seek, tucking up our skirts to jump over even the tallest walls.

The monsoon season was endless fun. The lake would fill up to the rim; the dam would be opened to save the town from a flood in case of more rain. What beautiful fish came along with the gushing water! We would catch them and drop them into wells, then check them at high noon to see if they were still alive, if they had grown any bigger. We would throw down puffed rice and watch them eat it. We would sit along the lakeshore in the evenings and chat. The banks would be full of December shrubs. We would gather the flowers, make a string of them, and divide it into equal lengths among us. There was a canal next to my house where we learned to swim. We would challenge each other to see how long we could stay underwater.

We would keep on playing even after we were soaked by the rain. We would go swimming in the canal. Vasumathi's mother would yell at us. "What do you think you are, senseless buffaloes? You're acting like boys. Keep on like that, and your ears will fall off."

There was an open well in the panchayat office compound. Once, after the rains, when we had gone to check the level of water in the well, Vasumathi fell in. Anna jumped in and saved her.

We would catch dragonflies and make them carry small stones, or tie strings on their tails and watch them fly around. During summer breaks it was butterflies. We would fill bottles with them. We would catch baby squirrels and keep them as pets. I kept one baby squirrel for a long time. How soft its fur was! It used to sit on my shoulder. It loved milk. I would dribble milk drop-by-drop into its mouth with my fingers, and watch it drink. One day Appa saw me with it on my shoulder, grabbed it by the tail and flung it away. He beat me as well. After Appa left, I fed the baby squirrel with water. It began to play again, as usual; I wasn't too badly hurt either, thank God. After that I gave the squirrel to Vasumathi. Vasumathi's parents didn't object; they doted on her.

During the summer holidays, we would hunt for plants, and bring them home and turn our homes into lovely gardens.

We could proudly claim that we had climbed every tree in the area. Whenever any fruits came into season, people used to fear us even more than the monkeys. We would sit on the trees and eat mangoes with salt and chili powder, and then run away before the owners woke up.

Once, we got caught at a neighbor's house. There was a tree there with wonderfully juicy mangoes. There was a huge wall between our houses; Anna and I would climb over the wall and pick the mangoes. When the neighbor noticed that the mangoes were missing, they fixed shards of glass into the top of the wall with cement. We picked them off, but one shard that we'd missed cut into my leg as we were climbing over the wall. My thigh was soaked with blood, but I felt no pain. I still have a long scar from my thigh to my foot.

The woman who lived next door was very upset about the disappearing pieces of glass. We would sit with her as she grumbled about it. She worried that if the thieves could pick out the glass pieces, they might also have knives to stab her with. We would just laugh to ourselves.

It wasn't only mango trees. We even climbed the towering palms. With sickles tucked in our skirts we would clamber up a palmyra tree to pick the cluster of *nungoo*s and suck out the soft middle. Once, on a palmyra tree, I was bitten by a fire ant, and started bleeding. I climbed down the tree in great pain and ran to Vasumathi's mother, who scalded my wound and burned the fire ant to ash.

I was a very good student. I used to write poetry. Because I was so scared of Appa, I used to write only when he was away. When I was in the tenth standard, Geetha fell in love with a boy from the next street. That boy started coming home every day. I would ignore them, and concentrate on my poetry. But someone told Appa about the boy, and he walloped me because I had known about it and hidden it from him.

At that time Anna was doing his higher studies, staying with my uncle in Bangalore. It was around that time that I attained puberty. When the same thing happened to Geetha, Appa held a big celebration, but for me he didn't even do as much as buy a new dress. Whenever he did buy new clothes, for Geetha, Anna, and Vatsala, he would get me something awful, not even as good as what he would buy for the maidservant.

Anita, my youngest sister, was born when I was in the seventh standard. She was Amma's ninth child. Five of us were born after she became mentally unstable; I was the first of those, and Anita was the last.

Geetha enrolled in Meenakshi College for pre-university. That boy she loved kept coming home.

Once, when I was thirteen, she dropped me at the Pallavaram railway station and disappeared for the whole day. I waited there for her until evening, missing school entirely. Finally the station master sent me home. Geetha had still not turned up. When I told Appa what had happened, I got another beating, as usual. After looking for her for a long time, they finally found her at that boy's house.

After that, Appa moved us from Krishna Nagar to Arumbakkam. He also declared that he was not going to pay for my schooling anymore; I would have to get by on my own. He enrolled Vatsala in Seva Sadan School in Chetpet. I had to throw a big tantrum in front of Amma, showing her my mark sheet, in order to get myself enrolled in the same school. But at the end of the year, I got the highest grade in my class on the final examination.

Generally speaking, fathers want their children to study hard, and do well in their lives. Somehow, my luck was different. I had to work constantly, or else I was beaten. Because of this I never touched my schoolwork when Appa was around. He once caught me studying for my final exam and burned all my school books. Even then, trusting to my memory, I managed to come in first in the class.

Anna had come home from Bangalore for the holidays. One day I found a strange thing on the table, something like a balloon. I was playing with it when Anna and Appa returned. Appa saw me playing with the balloon, and began smacking me around. Then Anna started yelling at Appa: "You're fifty-five years old, your wife has gone mad, and still you need your sex? How dare you beat up a young kid because of that?" As soon as Anna had spoken the whole house went berserk.

Appa used to abuse Amma, too—bang her head until her teeth broke and her face swelled up—just because she took my side. After the holidays, when Anna went back to Bangalore, our aunt and uncle began looking for a marriage alliance for Geetha. Worried that the men would be more interested in me than in Geetha, they kept me locked up.

They found two brothers. The elder brother refused to marry Geetha because the dowry was not enough. But the younger brother offered to marry me with no dowry at all. He even offered to pay for the wedding. But Appa told him he had no intention of getting me married.

It's true, Surya; I've never been married till now.

Geetha got married two years later, when she was twenty. The man she married was an alcoholic, a gambler, and had many other bad habits besides these. Geetha has a son now…

I started working when I was sixteen. I would wake up in the morning, finish the household chores, go to the typewriting institute, and then go to my job. Geetha and her husband lived with us. They fought constantly. One day, the fight got serious, and Geetha's husband stormed out of the house, never to return.

The landlord's son, seeing my plight, wanted to marry me. He told his father about it, and his father in turn told Appa. He asked to see all our horoscopes, so he could try to discover the reason for our troubles. Appa gave him the horoscopes. The landlord came back saying, "It is your daughter Avanthika's horoscope that is flawed; and I know a way to remedy the situation."

One night, the night of the new moon, when Anna was still in Bangalore, the landlord sent away his wife and son. Geetha woke me up at around eleven, and told me that Appa wanted me to come out. When I went out, they sent me into that man's house. Inside, he asked me to undress. Shocked, I demanded to know where his wife and son were; he told me that they were out of town. When I protested, the man called Appa and Geetha and told them, "She is refusing; so I'm helpless." Appa and Geetha started hitting and kicking me. I almost lost consciousness. At that point the landlord helped me up, sat me down, and said, "I have to take the mystical juice from you, and make it into a magic pigment. Then I will put the pigment into a talisman which will solve your Appa's troubles. Your Appa has given his consent."

Appa and Geetha left us, and the landlord shut the door again. "Usually, on a nuptial night," he said, "we would have milk and fruits to eat. I'll give you some biscuits, instead." He fed me something. I passed out. I have no recollection of what followed. I woke up around one o'clock in the morning. He showed me something white and pasty, spread onto a betel leaf; he said that he had taken that from inside me. Afterwards, he took the three of us up to the terrace and performed a puja. The next day he gave each of us a talisman. Because I refused to wear it, I was beaten by Appa.

The landlord's wife must have suspected something. Now she didn't want her son to marry me anymore. She eventually created a big enough scene that we had to shift our house again.

Appa always liked to talk to women. Amma caught him doing it once, and started wailing. I was just returning home from work when I came upon this scene at the doorstep, Appa talking to a woman while Amma wailed away. I went up to Appa and told him, "Amma doesn't like you doing this. So why don't you stop it?" He called me dirty names and hit me, in the open street, right in front of that woman. I blacked out. They admitted me in KMC. That's when my nervous problem got worse; now I've become a person who jumps at even the smallest noises. The doctor prescribed Cardinol, but I showed very little improvement. Anna came to see me; he was very worried about my health. Every time he went out, Appa would start clobbering me again. One day I swallowed twenty Cardinol tablets, and lost consciousness almost immediately. Anna found me in that condition, brought the family doctor home, and got me admitted in KMC again. I think I must have been unconscious for around ten days. After that incident, Anna and Appa did not speak to each other much. Still, every time Anna was not there at home, my beatings would continue. I wanted to die. I hated Anna for saving my life. I tried to stay away from home as much as possible. Aside from office, I spent all my waking hours at temple. Even Sundays I would spend in temples: Maangaadu, Thiruverukaadu, Kondrathur, and others. There I would cry out my sorrows.

It was on one such day that Aravindhan followed me home from Thiruverukaadu. The Sunday after that, while I was again at temple, Aravindhan came to our home to tell Appa that he wanted to marry me. When I got back home I got the usual scolding. I thought it just the normal routine, and kept quiet. It was only later that I understood something else was going on.

Two weeks later, Aravindhan came to my office. We spoke to each other. After a few days, we went to Mahabalipuram together. Because of the love he showered on me, I was willing to do just about anything he asked. And so, before long, I became pregnant with my daughter, Nithya.

When Aravindhan came to know that I was pregnant, he asked me to have an abortion. "Why?" I asked. "After all, we're going to be married."

"No," he said, "I cannot marry you." I came to know that my family had sent thugs after him to get him to leave me alone.

Once Appa found out I was pregnant, he told me that whether I married Aravindhan or not, I was no longer welcome in his house. I told Aravindhan: "I don't care if you're not going to marry me; I will not abort this child. You can just leave me alone. I'll move into a hostel."

I was chased away from home when I was five months pregnant with Nithya. Appa made sure that he took every paisa I had saved until then.

A friend of mine found me a place to live. "If you want, you can come and live with me," I told Aravindhan. "Otherwise, you can go your own way." He came to stay with me. On the next new moon night, I went to the jewelry shop, got myself a thali and a pair of toe-rings, came home, placed them in front of the Amman idol to bless them, and tied my thali myself.

It was after that that I came to know Aravindhan's true nature. Now it was his turn to abuse me. Even when I was in my third trimester, he kicked me around, and banged me against the walls. When I was on the way to the hospital for my delivery, he forced me to have sex with him.

Surya, I must tell you about this one incident that happened. It was ten days before my delivery. He said his mother was unwell, and that he had to go to visit her. His mother stayed in Vellore. (He did this often, claiming to visit his mother. I never met any of his relatives. He never took me along. He made excuses to stay away from me fifteen days out of every month. I didn't know his address in Vellore. He told me that he was doing his post-graduation at New College, and that he was a part-time Chemistry teacher in a school. In any case, it was all a mystery to me; I didn't let myself think about it too much.)

"I'll be gone for ten days, so I'll take you back to your mother's," he said.

I knew that wasn't possible, so I refused. The more I refused the more adamant he became.

I finally accepted, and left with him to my mother's house. Geetha refused to let me enter. "Whores aren't allowed here," she said. "You can go back to wherever you came from."

Aravindhan and Geetha began to fight. The curses that flew between them were too much for any human ear. I kept silent.

"Bitch, you'll stand in the streets without a thali once your husband is dead." Geetha's curse echoed through the streets.

Aravindhan didn't stay any longer. He brought me home and began kicking me around. I was torn to threads. It's a wonder that the baby was not affected.

Surya, how come these curses come true so soon? Just a year after Geetha cursed me that way, it became true. But I'll tell you about that later. Now listen to this.

Aravindhan disappeared again, leaving me alone. He returned after ten days with a bag of dirty laundry, claiming that he had completed his studies and had vacated the hostel. All through that day, nine months pregnant, I washed those clothes by hand. The women from the neighboring homes scolded me for it.

That night, Nithya was born. My friend and her mother helped me in the weeks that followed. Aravindhan kept on disappearing, and then suddenly reappearing to kick me and hit me and take away whatever little money I had earned. I had to secretly hide away cash to buy milk powder for Nithya. From the day I delivered Nithya, for almost twenty days, I had nothing to eat, Surya; nothing but water.

I was then an RTP in the postal department. So I didn't have any maternity leave. Come to think of it, I had no leave at all. I was like a daily laborer. I was paid two rupees seventy-five paise an hour for eight hours; that was my only income.

Not only that—I would have to go work in whichever post office they assigned me. Once, in a single month, I was shunted between eighteen post offices: Arumbakkam, Amanjikarai, Anna Nagar, Chetpet, Flowers Road, Park Town, Choolai, Kolathur, Veppery, Perambur Barracks, Kilpauk, Ayinavaram, Jawahar Nagar, Vyasarpaadi, Washermanpet, New Avadi Road, Purasawalkam, Tank Road.

The pay slips from all these places would be sent to the Park Town post office, and it was only then that my pay would be released. If the statement did not reach in time, I would have to call up the respective offices to chase my papers. Thus, I had to hop from post office to post office for my work, and then I had to do the same thing all over again to get my pay.

I spent eight years doing this, Surya.

Because I was a daily wager, I would always return home late. If Aravindhan had not come home yet, I would be safe. If he was there, he would start kicking me in the street, demanding, "How come you're so late? Who were you roaming around with?" I would be left sitting there outside the house with the baby, with a splitting headache, until late in the night. It was only after Mumtaj Aunty from the next house came and knocked on the door, asking Aravindhan to take me in, that he would relent. I wouldn't dare knock on the door myself, knowing that he would just kick me again. What kind of a life was this? Didn't I deserve a life like other women? The black magician when I was fifteen, all the abuse at the hands of Appa and Geetha, Mother's frightening madness... Had I escaped that hell just to get myself into this trap with Aravindhan?

Nithya was a year and a half old when Aravindhan contracted tuberculosis. I took him to the doctor.

(I forgot to tell you one thing that happened in the middle. When Nithya was six months old, I had gone to work in the charting office on a deputation. That was where I met Diwakar, who became my good friend. I told him my life story. I was there in that office for six months.)

Aravindhan's condition worsened. I had him admitted in the hospital. The doctor said that, along with tuberculosis, he had brain fever. I sent a telegram to Aravindhan's parents, asking them come down. They came, but they did not say a word to anyone.

The doctor said that Aravindhan needed a very costly injection. "How costly?" I asked. "Six hundred rupees," he said. I had only about twenty on me. Aravindhan's parents stayed silent. I knew I could not expect them to chip in. Then they started shouting at me, claiming that all this trouble was because of the second marriage.

Second marriage? I didn't understand, but I had no time to worry. I had to get the injection ready.

It must have been around five o'clock. I took an auto to a Seth's shop in Choolaimedu. I had nothing to sell except my thali. I took it off and pawned it for a thousand rupees. I took an auto back and inquired in every medical shop, but the medicine Aravindhan needed was nowhere available. I came to Apollo hospital. They had the right medicine, but they said it was not for sale, as they needed it for their own use. Finally, in Nungambakkam, I found a shop that had it in stock. By the time I reached the hospital, it was one o'clock.

In spite of giving him that costly medicine, there was no improvement. Aravindhan went into a coma. A friend of his said that we should get his photograph to use in a puja for him. I went back home, brought down the cardboard box from the loft, and started looking for a photo. That was when I got my shock. The box was full of love letters, photographs, and diaries. Going through the contents, I finally understood what Aravindhan's parents had meant. Aravindhan already had a family in Vellore.

I returned to the hospital. Aravindhan had regained consciousness. He held my hands and begged me, "Do anything, but save me! I know I have hurt you a lot. Forgive me. If I live through this, I will never leave you again."

"Of course you'll be all right. And you can live with whichever woman you want to. I promise."

He seemed happy. But he did not open his eyes again.

I sat at his feet, peacefully meditating.

May the soul rest in peace. May this man, who was so restless in life, at least find peace after death.

It was around two o'clock at night. His relatives took me and his body in a van. At Ega Theatre, on Poonamallee High Road, they dropped me off with Aravindhan's body, and left.

I still can't understand, Surya. Has this world gone so rotten? Why does everyone treat me like this? I have never hurt anyone. I have never even spoken harshly to anyone. So why am I being subjected to this?

While I was standing there alone on Poonamallee High Road, at the gates of Ega Theatre, my thoughts kept racing.

I had left Nithya with Mumtaj Aunty. That aunty was my only support.

I don't know how long I stood there with Aravindhan's body. It was only because an auto driver came that way that I'm even alive today.

Those people who left me alone with Aravindhan's corpse returned on the sixteenth day to take me back to finish the rituals. There was not a single woman in that crowd, only around twenty men. They said they were Aravindhan's cousins. I had never met any of them before. They said the rituals would take place in Amanjikarai. Seeing that I was scared, a neighbor's daughter offered to accompany me there.

The place looked like a lodge. Several strange rituals were performed. Finally they chopped off my braid—my long braid which reached down to my knees. Since then, Surya, I have never let my hair grow. I always keep it cut short. Before, I used to take the art of hair care very seriously. Now I couldn't be less bothered.

Once Aravindhan died I was left all alone. Anna came back and found me a house in Amanjikarai. There, too, my troubles continued. Aravindhan's family began demanding to take the child. I shifted to a house near my parents' place in Arumbakkam.

It was during this time that a problem arose at work. I had faced a similar one when I first started working. That was in a chemical factory; the owner was a man named Ramakrishna Iyer. I had a clerical job with a salary of 175 rupees a month. Ramakrishna Iyer tried to get funny with me, so I gave up that job after just three months, and joined an electrical shop as a typist. Later, I gave that up as well, to join as an instructor at the same typewriting institute where I had studied. I stayed there several years before I got this post as an RTP clerk in the Post Office, based on my marks in SSLC.

But the problem I had to face now was worse than those that I had faced in those private firms.

An officer by the name of Azhagesan had joined us. He was a womanizer. He found it convenient to keep me stationed in his office, rather than shunt me around from one place to another. He was the head of that office. "Let me come straight to the point. Let's have sex just once. And I'll give you anything you want," he said. Every time he said this, I would lower my head and leave the room.

But he wouldn't leave me alone. He constantly asked for files from my desk. My savior then was Inspector Srinivasan, at the next desk. Every time Azhagesan would call me to his room, Srinivasan would find some excuse to follow me there.

Such a high-ranking officer would actually wait at the bus stop, take the same bus I took, and follow me home. One day when Srinivasan was on leave, Azhagesan called me to his room, threw a gold chain on the table, and said, "This is for you. All you have to do is you say 'Yes,' just once." I ran out, sweating profusely. The next day, my colleague Savithri was showing off the same chain, saying she bought it with her savings.

One day, Azhagesan came to my father's house. Everyone at home was very thrilled that a higher official was visiting me. I kept saying, "He's a womanizer, don't let him inside." But they got angry with me. "Poor old man. What stories you tell about him! He's just being kind."

Do you know what that "kind" man did one Sunday? The postal service exams were going on. He asked me and Samikannu, the peon, to come along with him. When the exam finished, only Samikannu, Azhagesan, and myself were left in the office. I was preparing the list of those who had taken the exam. It started raining. It was only five in the evening, but the sky had become so dark it looked more like eight. I was hurrying through my work because I wanted to get home fast.

There was a bell from Azhagesan's room. Samikannu went in. When he returned he had a thermos in one hand and an umbrella in the other.

I was getting scared. What if Samikannu left to buy coffee? But Samikannu was a good man; he understood my thoughts. Besides Inspector Srinivasan, Samikannu was my second savior. Silently, he signaled to me: *Don't be scared, I'll be back in a moment.* As soon as he left, Azhagesan came out of his room and approached me. I got up, thinking, "It doesn't matter if it's pouring; I can run away." But by then Azhagesan was there at the main door, barring my way. I tried to figure out how to escape. Our office was on the first floor. I would have to get past Azhagesan to reach the stairs.

I don't know where I got the strength from, Surya. I shoved him aside and ran down the steps.

Samikannu came back and looked at both of us.

"Forget the coffee, get her an auto. It's getting dark," ordered Azhagesan. As I was getting into the auto, he said, "Madam is very nervous. Go along with her, Samikannu."

I replied, "I am not nervous. But Sir up there is very nervous. Please see that *he* gets safely back home." From the next day onwards, he stopped bothering me.

I would cry to myself: "All these problems are because I'm alone!" I would pray to the Goddess that she should come and save me. One day, these words rang in my ears: "Not to worry. There is someone to take care of you. You know him. He will come into your life soon."

As usual, I went to work the next day. Within a few minutes, I was told I had a telephone call. When I took the call, I was surprised. It was Diwakar! I told him about Aravindhan passing away. We met that evening. Diwakar said, "All through yesterday, I kept thinking about you. Some voice urged me to speak to you today. And that's why I'm here."

Surya, I know an atheist like you might find this surprising, but that is how it happened. Not just that; I forgot to tell you—even when I met Aravindhan in Thiruverukadu temple the first time, that same voice rang in my ears. What is surprising, Surya, is that I hear no voice about you.

Diwakar was up front with me. "I cannot marry you. You have a daughter, and therefore you will never be accepted in my home. But I promise to support you all through your life."

We became very close. Within a few short days, our relationship became a strong one.

Appa and Geetha kicked me around like a football. I told Diwakar about all this. The only place we could meet was my office. We could not live together; Diwakar was too scared to take me home.

It was around that time that my anni, my sister-in-law, died in a road accident. That is a separate story. Still, I shall tell it to you now.

They looked for a bride for Anna in different places. Several horoscopes were exchanged. Behind closed doors, a family from Nanganallur appealed to Appa and Anna, and got the alliance fixed. The horoscopes matched perfectly. The girl worked as a teacher. It was only after the marriage that we came to know about that family and the girl.

She would fight with Anna constantly. Perhaps because Appa had retired, he suddenly seemed to have become very old. His authority could not stand up against Anni's; she pushed him to the corner. Although she was the same age as me, she would hit me. If Anna took my side, that was it!

One day she was screaming horrible curses at Anna. The reason for the fight was this: she had been in love with another man before her marriage. It was to break that relationship that her parents had got her married to Anna.

My family is a family of lunatics. How could a woman marry into it and not go mad herself? Anni still had a relationship with her lover. He was her real life partner; my brother was just the public face. We couldn't do anything about it. She had already convinced her parents that we were abusing her and threatening to kill her. We couldn't say a single word to her without her family hearing about it.

One night there was loud shouting from Anna's room. Anna walked out. He told me this: she had insisted that he use a condom. Apparently he had asked, "I haven't used one until now, why should I use one tonight?" She had replied, "I want to become pregnant only by my lover, not by you."

Finally we came to know that she was already pregnant. She even agreed to have a D&C done. Do you know what the nurse told us in the hospital? "This is her fourth D&C. If she continues doing this, she'll puncture her uterus. Are you mad?"

We had no idea. Imagine how Anna must have felt.

When we returned from the hospital, her tantrums grew even more violent.

Do you know what she said to Geetha's son Vaasu one day? "Dey! You will be run down by a lorry on the street! Your head will be smashed in! There won't be enough of your body left for your mother to cry over—it will all be crushed into porridge!" Geetha had no word to say against her. We were stunned. Anna gave her a tight slap.

"I will not rest until I see you in prison!" she screamed. "If I don't hang myself right here in this house and land all of you behind bars, my name is not Kausalya!"

Vaasu must have been around seven years old when his aunt threw this curse at him. From that day on, every time he stepped out of the house, he had heavy security; two people in front of him and two behind. The entire household was expecting a huge misfortune to befall him. We felt as though we were enveloped in a curtain made of curses. We stopped speaking to each other. A fear of impending death threatened us all.

It was a Sunday, exactly seven days after Anni spoke her curse. It was seven o'clock in the morning. Anni was going out.

"It's a Sunday. Do you have to go and teach?" asked Anna.

"I don't need to answer your questions. Just drop me off on Hundred Foot Road."

Anna did not argue. He started the scooter and left with Anni. A little while later, Anna returned with this news: a lorry had come from behind and crashed into the scooter. Anna fell to the left, and Anni to the right, under the wheels of the lorry. Her head was smashed in. There wasn't enough of her body left to have a postmortem done—it had all been crushed into porridge.

Whatever was left of the body was on the doorstep, wrapped in a white sheet. Even the face was smashed beyond recognition.

Her elder brother came and stared at what was left of the face. He started tugging at her gold earrings. They would not come off. With no warning, he took a pen knife from his pocket and chopped off her ears.

And that was the end of my anni's life.

The next year, Geetha's husband, who had separated from her several years back, was burned to death in a factory fire. Not even a bone was left.

Once Anni was dead, Appa resumed control.

I cried to Diwakar, "I cannot take it anymore. I am going to die!" Diwakar found me a house in St. Thomas Mount. He introduced himself to the neighbors as my husband. But once I moved there, my nervous problem returned, along with epileptic fits.

I would lay there unconscious for God knows how long. My limbs would be spasming, my mouth foaming. Nithya would sit next to me, courageously, feeding me spoonfuls of water.

At that time Diwakar was working at St. Thomas Mount. His house was in Chinmaya Nagar. He didn't come home every day, except during holidays. I told Diwakar it was difficult to handle the child alone.

Anna had bought a house, also in Chinmaya Nagar. Diwakar spoke to him and I moved to the first floor of that house.

Diwakar's visits became more and more infrequent. Suddenly, one day, he came and announced that his mother had been diagnosed with uterine cancer, and so he could no longer refuse her wishes.

And that meant…?

He was getting married the next day.

It was much later that I learned that he did not get married to the girl whom his mother chose. It was a girl who worked along with him in the same office. The relationship had been going on for a long time.

I hate having to write this, Surya. Are you tired having to read it? How many times can the same thing keep happening to me?

And so my relationship with Diwakar came to an end. But living life is not as simple as writing it. I do not know if one lifetime is enough for the wounds that Diwakar and all the others inflicted on my heart, and my body, to heal.

Because Diwakar could not marry me, he did not want to have a child with me. Because of that I had to undergo D&C three times. I even tried Copper T. But the flow during my periods became so heavy I had to have it removed. With every D&C I thought I would die. I would keep chanting my slokas, crying my heart out. I felt like killing Diwakar. This, too, was a life. It might be a very tiny one—but once it was born and grew up, it would be a child, like Nithya. Would that child resemble me or Diwakar? Just because it hadn't yet been born, did I have the right to kill it? Is it right to kill a living being just for a few moments of sexual pleasure? My little baby appears in my dreams, and begs me: "Amma, please don't kill me, please don't kill me!" Does Diwakar understand this suffering? The letters "D&C" kill me every time I hear them. Delivering a child is a blessing. It is a birth of life; it is joy. One can put up with any amount of pain for the smell of a newborn. But *this* is death—no, it's murder. How many times can one commit murder? And having murdered, with whom do you share the guilt?

When I went for the third D&C, the doctor said, "It's only 30 days. It may still be in the tubes. Once I clean up the uterus, it may go in there. So wait for a few more days."

So I went after a few more days. She laid me on the table. Even as she was checking my blood pressure, I felt a pain inside me. When they gave me the tranquilizer, I wasn't able to go unconscious like the previous times. I was still half-awake.

The mouth of the uterus was dilated and I could feel the scraper enter it. Now it was scraping the walls of my uterus. Surya, I cannot describe the pain I felt; only a woman could understand that. I was bleeding profusely. That was the only time I ever I regretted being born as a woman. I wanted to die. I thought of all those women who, during their abortions, were not scraped fully, or who had the fetus stuck inside them as a mashed piece of flesh and had to undergo another D&C to have it cleaned again, or who had to have their uterus removed because it was damaged beyond repair. Some women even lose their mental balance during this experience.

I, too, had a bad session then. I had to go back to my doctor friend Jessy because I kept bleeding for a month non-stop.

I was still working as an RTP. My body had become a torn rag, and even as I bled, I had to keep up with office work. It was Jessie's care and love that saw me through that.

When you and I decided that we were going to marry, Surya, I asked Jessie, "Will I still be able to have a child?" She said she would have to do some tests. What will the test results be? Has Diwakar ruined my uterus forever? Will I never have the fortune of bearing of your seed in me? I don't know, Surya.

Remember, you told me once: "I don't need a child of my own. You and Nithya will be enough; when I have you two children, why would I need any more?" Surya, I love you, da.

Once, after I separated from Diwakar, I was coming out of the office holding Nithya's hand. Suddenly a speeding car rushed towards me. I grabbed Nithya close to me, but the car knocked me down. My head banged into a lamppost. I lost a lot of blood, and had to stay bedridden for two months.

How much can this body take? I went into a depression. You wanted to know what happens when one is depressed. It's like being drowned in the sea, the water weighing down on me. I lose control of my body. I can't understand anything you say to me. I can't even understand the words I say myself. My senses are somehow delinked from my brain. I'm unable to bear the pressure; I grind my teeth together, my hands and my face twitch involuntarily.

Anti-depressants give some temporary relief from this agony. But then they begin to rule my senses. It's impossible to manage without them, though. It would be impossible to sleep. My nerves would be completely shot.

But Surya, I did encounter one wonderful thing in my life. I have met you. I don't need my pills anymore. Since I met you, I don't get my fits. My depression has disappeared. Your love has been the medicine that has saved me.

After so much pain, finally my life has taken a turn onto a new, joyous path. I have left myself—my life—in your hands. You cradle me in your eye, scared to even blink lest you hurt me. That's enough for me. I have no more words to describe my happiness.

Yours,

Avanthika

P.S. I forgot to tell you about Vasumathi. After her wedding, she moved to Calcutta. Her husband was an engineer. I met her a year after her marriage. She did not want to return to Calcutta. She wanted to stay with her mother and get a job here.

Besides the usual problems with the parents-in-law, her husband's elder sister was also living there with them, along with her two sons. Her husband was employed in Dubai.

The problem was with the boys. Besides serving them, she also had to also suffer their slaps and punches. They didn't know how to feed themselves. One of them, when she went to feed him, pulled the plate out of her hand and threw it at her face. Her lip split open and there was blood. They both clapped their hands and jumped in joy. "Ah, blood! Blood!"

One day, while she was bathing, they locked her inside the bathroom. She had to stay there until her husband returned from work in the evening. He thought it was funny. When her parents-in-law returned in the evening and were told about it, they all laughed as if it were a huge joke.

On another day, the boys opened the gas cylinder. She barely escaped death that time. It was on that day that she finally demanded, "Why aren't these two put in a mental institution? Why do I have to put up with them?" That was it—the mother-in-law yelled back: "Are you calling my grandsons mad? Wait, I'll make sure that *you* end up in a padded cell."

I told Vasumathi not to return to that home. But Vasumathi's parents convinced her to go back to her husband. Within a year, the members of that house drove her completely insane.

The maid in Vasumathi's house was puzzled about a locked room there. Sounds of sobs and laughter would emerge from the room. One day, when no one was in the house, she looked through the keyhole.

Inside was a woman, naked, sitting in a corner. The maid rushed to the police station and made a complaint.

When the police arrived, Vasumathi was unable even to tell them her own name. The old hag and her husband said, "Our daughter-in-law has gone mad. If we let her out, she'll try to stab us with a knife." The police informed Vasumathi's parents, who brought her back.

Now all Vasumathi can do is point at her half-burned vagina, sobbing and trying to say something that no one can understand. She is being treated in a mental asylum.

The man whom she married, his sister, and his parents, have reduced her to this state in just two years. Why do such horrible things happen, Surya? Shouldn't a man celebrate a woman's body? How can he violate it like this? How beautiful Vasumathi used to be! I pray to my Goddess, even now, that she will someday recover.

0°

CHAPTER 33

"I'VE NEVER SEEN such a beautiful woman in Tamil Nadu before," Surya said, the first time he laid eyes on Avanthika. "You look like you must have just traveled over from Central Asia, across the Khyber Pass."

"I know what you mean. But I'm neither Aryan nor Mughal, and I don't believe in caste or religion. I'm just a woman."

"That sounds like a line from some Tamil movie."

Within a few short days, they decided to get married.

Avanthika wanted to have the wedding in a temple.

The only person who helped Surya with the wedding was his friend Nila Magan, "Son-of-the-Moon". Nila Magan was a pulp writer. He taught Surya that by sending any piece of invented gossip about movie actresses to a certain tabloid magazine, he could earn forty-five rupees, enough to buy his daily beer. Surya tried to keep this practice a secret, but it leaked out eventually. His circle of literati friends boiled over with righteous outrage that anyone could sink to such depths just for beer money. They all broke off their friendships with Surya. He was left with a single confidant, Thirumalai, to whom he confessed his love for Avanthika and discussed his plan to marry her. Thirumalai's response was, "Oh, get lost. Today you say Avanthika is the height of perfection, she's an angel. After nine months you'll be grumbling that she's a demon, that you were better off with Nalini, that you want another divorce. Then after the divorce you'll probably write another novel, *Gunfight Kanchana* or something, about your latest failed marriage, and force us all to read it. Why should *we* have to suffer?" After that, Surya never discussed his marriage plans with the literati set.

There was another reason to keep it a secret. The members of the literati set were all friends with Nalini, too. If they came to know about the wedding, the news would be sure to reach her. But he had to keep it a secret for nine more days.

The problem was this. The wedding couldn't be postponed for too long; Avanthika couldn't stay on anti-depressants forever. But the divorce still hadn't come through. He had given the court clerk a little bribe of ninety rupees to get to know the exact date when the divorce would be finalized, and had fixed the wedding for the following day. But a new coalition government had just taken over at the centre, and declared the birthdays of three political leaders and three visionary founding fathers as new national holidays. A weekend in between meant that the nation would come to a standstill for nine consecutive days. And so the divorce papers would come too late.

Thirumalai warned Surya that if he tried to get married without first getting the divorce finalized, he could be arrested under the bigamy law. Surya had sworn never to meet Thirumalai again, but had by chance bumped into him on the road, and Thirumalai had jumped at the opportunity to drop this bombshell on him.

He had been hurrying to meet Avanthika at the Museum Theatre when he happened to run into Thirumalai near the LIC building on Mount Road. Thirumalai had invited him for a beer. Even if he hadn't had an appointment with Avanthika, there was no way he would have accepted the invitation. He knew Thirumalai too well. As soon as he was fully drunk, he would start demanding: "You owe me 144 rupees—135 rupees for the beer plus 9 rupees for the boiled egg. No need to chip in for the 18 rupees I spent on cigarettes." Why bother to have a drink with such a cheapskate?

Surya still remembered the last drinking session they'd had. Between them they had polished off a litre of *Maha Muni* rum—Old Monk—when Thirumalai pulled a long face and began to calculate how much Surya owed him. The cigarettes, of course, were complimentary. Surya remembered clearly that they had ordered in quarter-bottles, and that he himself had paid for the first quarter. But Thirumalai denied it.

It irritated Surya no end that the evening's discussion, which had ranged widely over Althusser, Lévi-Strauss, Roland Barthes, Foucault, Derrida, and Deleuze, had now suddenly devolved into an argument about rupees, annas, and paisa. It was all the more annoying because he was quite certain that he had paid for the first quarter. He reminded Thirumalai that his memory had been failing recently; Thirumalai retorted that these days, there was no longer any need to hunt in the vegetable market for vallarai keerai to improve the memory; now it was easily available in capsule form. Surya felt that everyone was out to cheat him. His wife, his parents, his friends—everybody was just trying to swindle him out of everything he owned. *They all think I'm an idiot*, he brooded, self-pityingly. Surya was of the firm opinion that those who wallow in self-pity are lower than the worms that live in shit, so the fact that he was pitying himself only made him pity himself all the more.

He had sworn then that he would never join Thirumalai for another drink. So, that day on Mount Road when Thirumalai invited him for a beer, Surya refused.

"Okay. Let's have a smoke together, at least," said Thirumalai.

"Avanthika's waiting for me at Museum Theatre. I'm in a hurry."

"Hmm, what's this? You've given up drinks and cigarettes, have you? But you haven't given up lying. Your girlfriend is waiting for you at Museum Theatre, in this hot sun? If that's really true, then your life is made, man. Next you'll build a house, buy some sweaters. You'll become a typical middle-class guy," Thirumalai said knowingly, nodding his head. But what Surya heard was the string of curses behind these words: "May you be ruined, may they start preparing your funeral bier, may the pox take you." Surya took to his heels.

Thus ignored by the literati, and ignoring them, Surya was isolated. There was only Nila Magan left to help with the wedding preparations. When Surya first came to know him, he did not like Nila Magan very much. What crazy sort of a name was Nila Magan, anyway? But after a while, Surya began to find his idiotic antics endearing.

He was funny. Nila Magan would write twenty-seven-week serialized stories for popular magazines, and accept the nine hundred rupees they'd pay him with gracious servitude. The magazine even once ran a state-wide advertisement for his story with color posters featuring a photograph of his smiling mug.

Nila Magan had thirty-six girlfriends that Surya knew of. Some were married, some unmarried, some widowed, some divorced, college students, lady doctors... an astounding variety of women. *I need to have sex with you. At the very least, I need to kiss you. I'm still dreaming about the last kiss you gave me, on September 27th. My eldest son is in the ninth standard. I can't forget the last time we had sex—I've never felt so happy.* Such were the love letters Nila Magan would receive from his girlfriends. It made Surya want to get into writing detective fiction, too.

Surya thought about his stale literary world, all the boring seminars in which he participated. Once, standing in front of a microphone, it had struck him. "There are no women here. It looks like the meeting of a **gay club**. I don't feel like talking," he had said into the microphone, and sat down. He barely escaped with his life that evening.

Surya often regretted that his chosen field was so devoid of women. The few women who did show up to the seminars made him *want* to become a member of a **gay club**. Or else they were terrorists, equipped with meat cleavers, eager to chop off the dicks of the men around them to avenge their anger. He felt a great weariness in his heart at being stuck in such a dangerous field. But Surya had a bad habit of never being able to give up his habits. And doing the literary thing was a habit.

Nila Magan took the time to answer every piece of fan mail he received. Surya found that most surprising. He thought of Vazhipokkan, editor of *Prabanja Kaalam*, who had sent him sixty-three post cards asking him to translate a short story of Kothgasser's for his journal—all of which he had studiously ignored. (Vazhipokkan is still writing him these postcards... but that's another story.)

Nila Magan engrossed himself in the wedding arrangements. Mindful of Thirumalai's warnings about bigamy and arrest, they kept everything a close secret. Surya told the temple authorities not to register his marriage because he didn't have the divorce papers yet. The temple authorities said they wouldn't allow an unregistered wedding. But Nila Magan got in touch with a friend of his, the editor of a big magazine, who intervened and solved the problem. "It's in cases like this where it helps to know a few influential people," said Nila Magan. "You're right," Surya agreed.

Next, the stress of finding a house to rent and gathering all the money for the wedding expenses resulted in Nila Magan having a mild heart attack. That meant twenty-seven days of total bed rest.

Then came the wedding day.

Surya had told none of his literary friends, but had invited his relatives, and Nila Magan's friends.

Surya had given his mother money to buy a thali. But his parents were late for the ceremony, so he sent Nila Magan's friend to buy another thali. Just as the friend left, his mother and father arrived.

"Hee hee, we stopped for tea. That's why we're late," said his father.

"First give me the thali," Surya said, almost snatching it out of his mother's hands.

Thirumalai's words were ringing in Surya's head. *Bigamy! Arrest! Bigamy! Arrest!* Even as he tied the thali with trembling hands, he imagined Nalini gatecrashing the wedding with a pack of police like a Tamil film heroine and having him arrested.

When he had confessed this fear to Avanthika that morning, she had said, "If anything like that happens, and you have to go to prison, I'll kill her myself and end up in the prison even before you do. Don't worry about such things!" But it had only made him more terrified.

"What is this? Why spoil such a happy occasion by talking about things like murder and prison? We should be celebrating now!" said Surya.

But he could not stop imagining himself and Avanthika behind bars in separate prisons. He remembered that Thirumalai was the cause of all these anxieties, and that made him even angrier.

None of Surya's fears materialized. The only unexpected thing that did happen was that The Honorable Tamil Writer had heard about the wedding and decided to attend. "Congratulations, Surya!" he complimented him. "You have successfully Brahminized the entire Gounder culture!" Surya did not know what to reply. Nine days after the wedding he finally got the divorce papers from the court. Only then did he stop panicking about prison.

"I want to gift you with our child," said Avanthika.

"Please don't say that. *You* are like my child. Why go for another?" Surya asked dramatically. But Avanthika would not listen. She became pregnant, and then he too started eagerly awaiting the child's birth.

But the fetus was miscarried. Avanthika had to go in for D&C. "We don't need to have a child," said Surya. "You are all that's important to me." This time Surya really meant it. But Avanthika wouldn't listen. She believed that some strenuous work had caused the miscarriage, so the next time her pregnancy was confirmed, she refused to allow Surya to come near her, and avoided all strenuous work.

She miscarried again. Doctor Jessie, who did the second D&C, called Surya aside, and pointed out various features of the smashed fetus.

Avanthika wept for nine days after the miscarriage. "I wanted to take a bit of both of us, and make a child for you, Surya. Now my womb has become a burial ground for your baby," she wept.

TORCH panel, toxoplasmosis, Rubella, anti-sperm antibody, Chlamydia antibody—all kinds of tests were done, and all of them turned out positive. Jessie confirmed that the problem was a virus.

"Will I be able to have another child?" sobbed Avanthika.

"Chee, chee! Come on, don't cry like a baby. You're an educated woman. These days there are medical treatments for all this. The virus can easily be cured," said Jessie, prescribing more drugs.

Just as they were stepping out of the clinic, Diwakar walked in, along with his new wife, her arms covered to the elbows in colorful vallaikappu bangles.

0°

Chapter 34

THE LETTER FROM Muniyandi's girlfriend in the Rwandan drama troupe, and the papers just given to me by the wandering ascetic, seem to contradict each other. The girlfriend claims that Muniyandi died in Rwanda. But here are handwritten notes showing that he met with this ascetic in the Himalayas. I couldn't get any more information out of the ascetic; he had taken a vow of silence. He informed me, signing with his hands, that he had stopped speaking many years ago. He looked like the physical embodiment of silence. Time had etched deep lines into his skin. His body was thin and dessicated. There was a light in his eyes that pierced my heart. I felt a strong desire to remain in his presence for as long as I could. But he simply handed me the sheaf of papers and disappeared.

0°

NOW FOR THE LETTERS TO MY DAUGHTER

MY DEAR GENESIS,

It must be Fate that is stopping me from meeting you or talking to you, compelling me to write letters instead. I don't know when you'll get this letter, or who will deliver it. Being separated from you is too hugely painful for me to think about anything else.

A scene from the *Mahabharatam*: Bhishman and Arjunan are fighting. Then Arjunan sends a volley of questions to Bhishman. "This is not the time for questions," says Bhishman. "Turn your words into missiles. We will converse through our missiles, rather than through our words." Oh Genesis, I have forgotten your smell. Until recently, every time I thought of you, your smell would surround me, suddenly, from nowhere. But time has stolen it away from me. This letter is the only thing I have left. I have only language.

It was wonderful to think of you on this Christmas day, here, among Christmas trees. That wonder inspired me to write my very first poem.

> Frozen time.
> Numb universe.
> Mountains, trees.
> Nature's undisturbed meditation.

Guns' and bombs' destruction.
Land, water, air.
A boy selling sundal on the beach.
What saambaar and rasam shall I make today?
Okra fry? "Chee, what nonsense is this?
Does it have to be the same every day?"
She could hear her husband shouting.
A middle-aged woman
at the LIC bus stop, boarding the 1G.
God silently humming
his requiem for the death of mankind.
Somewhere in the distance a tiny sparrow
is translating that requiem for me.
Mind
yearning to leap from the ledge.
Violet and maroon flowers
like babies' laughter.
God stops his requiem.
Angels descend from heaven like snow.
The cold penetrates the marrow.
A bearded man was asked, "What
is the philosophy that will last to the end of the world?"
The bearded man answered, "Leave alone *my* philosophy,
no philosophy will last that long...
except Beethoven's **Fifth Symphony**."

The **Fifth Symphony**,
long forgotten by communists,
is being hummed by these Christmas trees.

That face might seem beautiful to you and me, but it irritated that little boy no end. It made him want to puke. The face haunted him in his classes, and he stopped going to school. He took whatever work he could find. He got a job as a daily laborer in a factory, and started writing poetry in his spare time. He was arrested because his poems were anti-national. His background was checked. The judge was surprised that such a good poet had no formal training in literature. "God sends me my poems from up above," he explained. The workers coalition was infuriated by this answer, and he was exiled.

God has sent me this poem today, Genny…

We came to this mountain yesterday. There were seventy-two hairpin turns on the road here. At each turn, there were signboards that read THE WAGES OF SIN IS DEATH. Surya wanted to get down; I could hear the distress in his voice. We hiked up a mountain path and lost our way. But the beauty of the forest calmed Surya's fears. The flowers on the jackfruit trees were in various stages of bloom. We wandered this way and that, and finally came upon some rocks, and sat down. From somewhere came an apocalyptic noise. We turned around in surprise to see a giant swarm of bees rushing towards us. We lay flat on the ground. When the bees had passed, we tried to find our way again. There was a hamlet in the distance. The way down the slope to the hamlet was thick with pineapple shrubs; the thorns tore at our legs. We were faint with hunger. We asked a passerby where the nearest hotel was. He said the closest was in the next village, a long way off, but that the guava tree there was his, and that we were welcome to pick as much fruit as we wanted from it. Once we had eaten the guavas, Surya asked him if there were any rice trees in the forest. The man laughed, and told us how to get to the village where the hotel was. But when we reached the hotel, they were out of meals. We asked for omlettes, and ate those.

We rested well and set off to a nearby waterfall—a deep gorge between mountain peaks that touched the sky. We had to go down the gorge before we could see the cascade. There were 720 steep steps to get there. The torrent seemed celestial, as though it was falling from the heavens. The place was totally uninhabited. To reach the waterfall we had to swim a ways. What a roar, what a tumult! I held onto a rock and stood under the fall. Ecstasy! Delirium! Experiential wisdom! When I stepped out of the waterfall, I was encircled by a rainbow.

I was never once away from you until you were nine, Genny. If I had to go out of town on work, you would whisper, with tears in your eyes, "Appa, I'll be thinking only of you." And I would cancel my trip. Instead, we would play Alisha on the stereo and dance.

Trying to escape these suffocating memories of you, I tried reading the *Ramayanam*.

When he is asked, "Why do you sleep all the time?" Kumbhakarnan answers: "I choose to sleep because I cannot bear all this injustice. I cannot surrender to Raman, as my younger brother has done. Whether I am to live or die, I will do it at my elder brother Ravanan's side."

On the battlefield, Kumbhakarnan realizes that the moment of reckoning had come. Raman comes to him and says, "I will give you anything you desire. Ask." Kumbhakarnan says, "It should never be said that I was defeated. Slice off my head with your arrow, and drop it in the ocean. Do not let go of it here on the battlefield. And if my younger brother Vibheeshanan ever abandons you, the way he has abandoned our elder brother, do not use your arrows on him. He will not be able to face it. Let him go. Spare his life."

Can that kind of unconditional love exist in today's world, Genny?

0°

Genesis, My Dear Little Princess...

My love for you is torturing me Genny... like this cold...

Since Misra came without a reservation, he couldn't get a train berth. So we made the arrangement that he would sleep half the time, and I would sleep the other half. He had brought his walkman along, and we listened to Kenny G, Richard Clayderman, and Eric Clapton for a while. The second night of the journey, in the wee hours of the morning, at Jhansi station... we were chilled to the bone. Our toes and fingertips felt like icicles. The cold penetrated even our cheeks, our earlobes, our foreheads.

Many years later, as he faced the firing squad, Colonel Aureliano Buendía was to remember that distant afternoon when his father took him to discover ice. Death and fire, memory and ice. This chill called for a cigarette. Misra went to the stall on the platform and asked the shopkeeper, "*Vills hai?*" "*Vills nahi hai,*" replied the shopkeeper. "What a language," Misra grumbled. "It sounds like he's got a bad toothache." Misra hates his own mother tongue. "Have you heard?" I asked him. "The IP College girls speak good Hindi."

Not able to find a cigarette, Misra finally fell asleep. I stood. After some time a stranger came and asked me if I wanted a smoke; I nodded. He even lit it for me. Perhaps cold weather reduces the distance between humans.

A short time passed. Gwalior station. Tea in clay matkas. With each sip came the smell of mud. I felt as though I had entered the womb of the Earth.

Again, thoughts of you took over. From the moment the nurse placed you in my arms in the delivery room, until you were nine, I never let go of you, Genny. Maybe that's why I'm not able to bear this separation.

I don't want to talk to anyone. So instead, I've got hold of some paper and I'm writing to you. Genny, I think the entire human race has given up on love and caring, and is headed for ruin. The nations divide themselves with armies along their borders. Man uses various survival techniques to protect himself, invisible weapons to hurt his fellow man. Aandal's lyrics ring in my ears:

As the candelabra burns, He slumbers, on a diwan with legs of ivory
Resting His head on Nappinnai's soft bosom
Flowers woven in her tresses, she woos Him:
"O broad-chested Lord, kindly speak!"

The fragrances of camphor and lotus;
How can they compare to the sweetness of those coral lips?
O white conch from ocean's depths, please tell me
Of the transcendent taste and fragrance of Madhava's mouth!

All conchs are white. So why call it a white conch? You must listen to the harikatha of Velukudi Varadhachariyar, Genny. He says Kannan's lips are so red that when the white conch rests on them, its whiteness is intensified.

"I will lie prostrated here for eternity for a glimpse of those coral lips. If I am not able to climb up the mountain, then I will become the very steps, in order to see those coral lips against the frozen snow," Velukudi Varadachariyar exclaims, melting with devotional ecstasy.

Now a different story comes to mind, that my friend Thirumalai once told me.

> A man came to Perumal and demanded, "Dey, Ranga! When am I going to get my nirvana, Ranga?"
>
> "How can I give you nirvana?" replied Perumal. "To attain nirvana requires knowledge, faith, and karma. You have absolutely zero knowledge, zero faith. As for karma, you even dare to disrespect me, calling me *Dey*. How can I send you on to nirvana?"
>
> "Dey, Ranga, Ranga, do I really have to explain this to you? Listen, let me tell you a story. A very rich man announced that he was going to give away all his gold coins to the poor. Every poor person came, carrying winnows, pots, and sacks to have filled with gold coins, except for a lone man who came empty-handed. 'Why haven't you brought anything to carry the gold?' asked the rich man. The empty-handed man replied, 'Aiya, you are giving us real gold. Can't you give us something to carry it in, as well?' I say the same thing to you, Ranga. You're going to gift me the priceless nirvana. So don't start demanding that I have the knowledge to understand it, the faith to believe in it and the karma to achieve it. Just gift it!"

I lack that depth of faith Genny. I live in an age deprived of God, love, and faith.

Humans and their doctrines terrify me, just as much as if I had landed on Earth from another planet.

I have no idea where I am headed on this journey. I don't know if I will ever see you again.

The train speeds along.

0°

My Little Princess Genny,

I have reached Delhi. I had a cold-water bath and set out for a walk in **zero visibility**. Around me everything was white with fog. Some pavement dwellers were warming themselves by a fire made from wood and dry leaves. I stood with them, warming my hands.

For some reason, a poem by Vannadhasan popped into my head. I couldn't remember the exact words, only the essence. A man with a fortune-telling parrot called out, "My parrot knows how to speak." Parrots don't speak. A bird's nature is to fly. Why does a chick born to a caged parrot have wings?

I walked to Connaught place. I liked the soundlessness of the atmosphere. All along the way I saw people walking around biting into raw white radishes. I walked up to the radish vendor. He scraped the radish, slit it, rubbed masala powder and squeezed lemon onto it before he gave it to me. Now I too was walking around biting into my radish, like the rest. There were a few policemen around a car at Regal Cinema. Inside the car there were some people eating something off a paper plate. "How can you park your car in such a busy place? Give me your license," said a policeman. They replied, "We are hungry, Saab, so we are eating." They continued to argue. Finally a man in the car said melodramatically, "Saab, see, I'm holding the plate in this hand and I'm eating with the other. How can I pull out my license? In the time I've spent arguing with you, I could have finished eating. I'm sorry we wasted your time; we'll be done and off in a minute." The policemen laughed and walked away. Just at that moment a mahout came by with his elephant. A silk cloth, twisted into a rope with bells tied to the ends, hung over its back. As the elephant moved the bells went *tun, tun*.

I remembered a Kalidasa poem that Thirumalai had told me—no, not a poem, a story. Actually, I'm not sure if it's really by Kalidasa. Thirumalai has been known to mix up authors.

> The poets in the court of King Boja, jealous of the friendship between the king and Kalidasa, challenged him to prove his mastery of words by completing the line: *Tun, tun, tun, tadun, tun...*
>
> Kalidasa said, "Oh King Boja, your lover is just climbing up the steps of the tank after her bath, in her wet clothes, carrying a pot of water, when she sees you. Surprised and happy, but also bashful, she lets go of the pot, which goes rolling down the steps of the tank: *tun, tun, tun, tadun... tun*. But, my dear King, I cannot say for sure what the meaning of that last *tun* is; you alone can tell us. Is it the sound of the pot falling upright on the last step, or is it the sound of her losing her heart to you forever?"

Every day, little girl, I think of the Taj Mahal. I remember that morning well. I was shaving. You were just waking up. Your first question to me was, "Appa, when will you die?"

Not expecting such an assault so early in the morning, I turned sharply, and blood appeared on my cheek. "Why do you ask, my dear?"

You said, "When you die, I want to build a Taj Mahal for you."

Do you remember, Genny? What can I give you in return for that love, my dear?

And what about that time you started crying because you didn't want to go out and buy cigarettes for your mother's male friends? My heart broke for you, my dear.

0°

To My Little Princess:

Nights here in Delhi are always extraordinary. The night before last we walked from Ashoka Hotel to Karol Bagh—around nine kilometers. Then last night, we went for a dinner at Pragati Maidan with around 450 old men and women. A few starlets were hanging around spilling artificial smiles for the crowd and having their photos taken. Surya, though, stood outside the maidan; he was not allowed inside. I told him I'd go in, procure an extra invitation, and send it out for him. I did, but he still didn't come inside. So I came back out again. When I asked him why he was being such a pain in the ass, he told me a story from the *Mahabharatam*.

"During the period of their exile, the Pandavas have to get across a pond. A Yakshan is standing guard over the pond. 'In order to cross over this pond, you must answer my questions correctly,' he tells them, 'otherwise, you will drown.' Except for Dharman, all the other Pandavas, confident of their powers, ignore the warning, step into the pond, and are drowned. Dharman alone comes forward to hear the questions, and answers them all successfully. The Yakshan, pleased, promises to give Dharman anything he wants. Dharman asks for Sahadevan to be brought back to life. The Yakshan is surprised and asks, 'Why would you ask not for your own full brothers, but for your half-brother?' To which Dharman replies, 'Of the sons born to my mother, I am still alive; so that a son may remain for my step-mother, I ask for Sahadevan.' The Yakshan, impressed with Dharman's selflessness, brings all the other Pandavas back to life. At the time of Dharman's conception, his mother Kunti was thinking about Yaman; nobody can ever defeat Yaman, and therefore nobody can defeat Dharman, either. The Yakshan at the pond, too, was Yaman.

"And among our group, it is you who are Yaman," Surya said. "I gave the invite you sent out to the others in our group."

We left the party and took the bus to Munirka, near JNU. It was midnight. We asked every car that passed us for a lift but nobody would pick us up.

It was cold enough to freeze the blood. Had humans lost all capacity to care for others? "If only Dostoevsky had come by in his car at this moment, he would have said 'Forgive me my friends, had I come earlier you would not have had to struggle so much. Tell me where you want to go, and I'll take you there.' Wouldn't he have?" said Surya.

A few days back we went to Kasi. I will never forget that Chamundi Temple for as long as I live. That huge scorpion, with its stinger piercing the stomach of the Goddess! It seemed to me that all the sorrows of the millions of women of India were reflected in her eyes.

We were eating at a *dhaba*. Misra wanted curd. The dhaba did not serve curd. So Misra gave nine rupees to Chotu, the young helper, and asked him to go buy some. Chotu took the money and left—forever. He never came back. We figured maybe he had gone to see a film. But the next day, the kid still hadn't come back. The dhaba owner and the cook laughed at us. "So, you gave nine rupees, and chased away our Chotu! Maybe he's bought a ticket back to his home town with those nine rupees. The poor *bechara* will be starving there. At least here, he used to get *rotis* three times a day," the cook told us. "Looks as though freedom is cheap! Only nine rupees!" The cook asked us if we would tell everybody back home in Chennai about being cheated by Delhiites. I told him not to worry. Then the cook told us his story. He had been in Chennai for nine months, living on a daily wage of ninety rupees. But he couldn't manage there. He said people were too serious. "There's no place like Delhi," I said. "*Delhi to dilwale ka hai!*"

Perhaps you remember it, Genny. You were there with me then, studying in the first standard. Once, after you had just visited your mother's house, you came to me crying and begging for a Michael Jackson cassette. Your mother loves music. She'll play music all day: Pandit Jasraj, Mallikarjun Mansoor, Dagar Brothers. I can just imagine her reaction when you asked her for Michael Jackson. "What vulgar music!" she would have exclaimed with distaste. Then she gave your cheek a brutal pinch. The marks from her fingernails were still there on your cheek! How are you managing there now?

I came to your crèche to see you, but you were absent that day. I met you there the next day. With your eyes full of fear, you kept whispering: "Come when Amma is here, come when Amma is here!" Seeing you, my little chatterbox, transformed into a trapped mouse like this—it made me cry. The next day your mother called to yell at me. "How dare you come to see her when I'm not there!" I wanted to try to get help from the courts so I would be able to visit you, speak to you. But your mother's friends kept on threatening me. I lacked the strength to battle those rowdies. But I couldn't *not* see you, either. That, Genesis, is why I began wandering around like a nomad.

Though my experiences have repeatedly taught me that simple, natural love between human beings is impossible without power trips, expectations, and demands, I still search again and again for love, like Vikramadithyan's vampire.

The **Desperado** soundtrack is playing. The piano and saxophone duet brings tears to my eyes. My world, filled with memories of you, slowly disappears. Only the sax reminds me of your voice. Genny, do you remember that your music master once said your voice was like a flute?

Genesis, more precious than my own life... what must you think of me now? Do you suppose that I've forgotten you, now that it's been so long, and I've gotten married again? No! Your new mother, Jennifer, says that I speak about you in my sleep. (I have renamed her Jennifer, for you.) It saddens her that she has still never seen her only daughter. Whenever I'm in Chennai, I call you every evening. There is no reply. I know that the house is locked and you are at the neighbors'. But I never call at night, lest your mother answers the call. I don't want to have another dogfight with her. So I just keep calling in the evenings, hoping someday you might answer, and I might be able to hear your voice.

The editor of that magazine accused me of faking all this distress, saying that I was now comfortably remarried and had forgotten you. I didn't reply to the accusation. Typical; people always scoff at the sorrows of others. Only Jennifer knows about my longing for you, and the threats that come from your mother.

I remember that summer when you and I were living by ourselves. You had chicken pox and the heat was intolerable. You wept—you *wailed*. You rolled around in pain. I never knew chicken pox could be so painful. As you rolled, the boils broke and the water leaked out of them. I cried, too, for your pain. You told me, "Appa, it's even worse when you cry." So I stopped. I asked you to think of God. "*You* are my God," you said.

Last year I didn't see you on your birthday. I didn't even try. It was the first year I missed it. I didn't want to make you face your mother's rage on that special day. Instead, I came to your crèche the day before. Strangely anxious, you claimed you didn't want a gift. You! You, who used to demand that I give you airplanes and ocean liners! Today you wanted nothing! When I insisted, you told me your mother had threatened to brand your thigh if you accepted anything from me. "I'll deal with your mother," I said. "Tell me what you want." Hesitantly, you asked for a pair of anklets. I immediately went out and bought you anklets for your golden feet. But the next day I got threatening phone calls from your mother and her women's association, and I couldn't go to give them to you. So the anklets are still with me.

Unable to wish you a happy birthday, and with your anklets weighing me down, I drank. I'm normally a moderate drinker, but that day I got good and drunk. At nine that night, I called up a poet friend of mine and moaned to him for forty-five minutes. He offered to go and wish you a happy birthday on my behalf. I never asked him if he actually did it. I don't think I have the strength to hear him say no.

It was this same poet friend who first told me the story of Sukran. We had been trekking all over Tamil Nadu together; after endless wandering we ended up in Kumily, where we had a friend. We took the friend along and went into the Thekkady forest, and that's when my poet friend, while piss-drunk, told me the story of Sukran and his extraordinary love for his daughter Deivayani. The next day, sober, he told the story again, and then explained what had triggered him to tell it in the first place; he said my love for you was as great as Sukran's love for his daughter. On another occasion, when I repeated my friend's comparison to Thirumalai, he ridiculed me, saying it was all a bunch of sentimental mush.

I remember a morning when I came to meet you, back when your mother was still respecting my court-ordered visitation rights. I had spent the previous night at a friend's place so I could get up and see you early. In the morning I lit a cigarette and left. A bus with no passengers came out of nowhere and sideswiped me, knocking the cigarette out of my hand. I escaped death by a hair's breadth. Shaken, I decided to travel on foot, and to my great surprise there you were, walking alone down the deserted road. That vision is still fresh in my mind. I asked you where you were off to so early, all by yourself. You smiled and said, "I'm just walking." I remember how we used to always go for a morning walk at Nageshwara Park in Mylapore. Do you still go for morning walks, Genny?

"When my spirit exits my body, will my body still be mine, or not?" asked Villiputhoorar. I think of that now. Karnan has fallen on the battlefield. Krishnan comes to beg for all of Karnan's dharma as alms. Then Karnan says, "I know not whether my life is still meshed in my lungs, or whether it has already flown away; what can I give you now?"

Neither do I know whether my life is still in me, or whether it has flown away. Or whether it's hidden in the crevices in the rocks of the mountainous memory of you, Genny …

Memories of us together hang like nocturnal bats in the dark canopy of my mind. I can only attempt to sketch them as poems.

Do you know the story of Thilothama, Genesis? She was created by amalgamating sesame-seed-sized pieces of all the wondrous things in the world. A child's lisp, the fresh foaming toddy drawn at dawn from a palm tree, a Bloody Mary, the receding sea, a dew drop clinging to blade of grass, a glint of sun reflecting off the dew, the third day crescent moon, the solitude of a moonlit night on a terrace, sparrows on a telephone line, clouds hugging you on the mountain peak, a deer's fearful eyes, a tailor bird's lonely call, the bells of a bullock cart, the far-off sound a of waterfall, a star, the silence of the forest, the summer rains, the smell of the soil—Dalí, when did you do your first painting? *I drew my first painting on the walls of my mother's womb*—a lover's first touch, breast milk; these and many, many more wondrous things were used in the making of my Genesis.

I want to scatter the stars and play jacks with you, kick the moon and play tag with you, twist the air into a rope and swing you on it, make the sky a net and fish with it, suck up the sea and spray it on your face till you're breathless, Genny…

Genny… my Little Princess… right now, my memories of you are destroying me, I'm destroying myself, it's driving me mad, Genesis...

I write you letters every day. Then I throw them in the dustbin. Once in a while I mail them. But I gather from what you tell me that your mother has made sure they still reach the dustbin safely. When I asked you if you ever received any of my letters you said no. So I think I'll give this letter to Nano. She'll make sure you get it.

I think the only possible relief from this torment of memory is death. If only I could destroy my memory, lose myself in silent nothingness…

Along with this letter I enclose my poems, but none of them are really mine. They are just borrowed words that have become poems because of your love, your lies and your laughter.

0°

For so many days I've watched you in the sky
making circles around me
and playing.
I get closer, hoping to catch you.
You run on in wider circles,
binding me in your magic,
dancing with glee,
clapping and laughing.
The expanse between you and me;
when will we bridge it?

who's that prankster
that plucked the stars out of the sky
and scattered them here on the Earth?

0°

METATONGUE

"The language is trapped in a bottle.
We've got to set it free somehow—
but without breaking the bottle!"
                              you said.
"It's already dead,"
                    I said.
"Rotted by maggots,
it just leaked out."
The loss of life
melts your heart.
"There must be some other way,"
                         you said.
I was confused,
but you went silent after that.
Poetry is the language language speaks,
and silence is the language you speak.
Now:
A small scotch and Kenny G on the stereo.
I'm lonely.
This world
is full of
seas rivers
trees humans
and air.

0°

words make
life
words make
love
words make
language
words make
poetry
words make
lifebreath
words make
tears
words make
the milky way
words make
sex
words make
friendship fear affection belief betrayal
hunger starvation murder blood suicide flesh
phlegm jealousy pus sacrifice chastity lust pain
seduction ardor wisdom joy ecstasy
sorrow madness illusion art war philosophy
light knowledge beauty darkness sky

words make
the voice
words make
the nipple
words make
the thin line of hairs drawn down from the navel
impassioned wet lips
green veins in the eye
ass spit forehead eyebrow cheek
cum-taste hair eye-gunk
shoulder thigh mole armpit tip of the nose lines
of the palm curve of the waist back earlobe
ankle dimple finger wrist
foot nape of the neck
words make words make
words make
words make
the Word

0°

outside my window there is no ocean there are no stars there are no clouds there is only the silent cemetery overflowing with nothingness the plant i bought you as a gift hoping you would visit on my birthday told me that my name is inscribed on a headstone there in the cemetery and then the plant died i keep watering it over and over trying to revive it as the leaves drop off i continue to water it i am obsessively watering a dead plant my friend laughs my life is vacillating between death and madness my eyes are searching through the window bars for the headstone with my name on it...

0°

On the porch under the tiled roof
of the house scarred by tradition,
a large
green frog
sat glaring at him.
He tried to wave it away
but that stupid frog
could not understand his sign language.
He trapped it
under a plastic mug.
Is the frog aware,
as it hops up and down
inside the mug,
that the man has killed two serpents?
That a third serpent escaped, wounded,
and is even now seeking
its vengeance?

0°

A TRAVELER MEETS
THE PRINCESS OF THE SHADOWS

In the market
at the edge of time,
a traveler asked the multi-shadowed
Little Princess,
"Give me a shadow."
"There are many shadows.
Pick the shadow
that suits you,"
the Little Princess said
with a smile.
"I want a shadow
that has the fragrance of your hand,"
begged the stranger.
"What does a traveler want
with a corporeal identity,
a memory's fury?"
asked the Little Princess.
"As soon as I answer that question,
my journey will come to an end,"
pleaded the stranger,
"and until then,
I need a likeness of your shadow."

"You'll have to explain that
to the original,"
said the Little Princess,
wringing her hands.
"The music you love,
the poem you love,
the flower you love,
the friend you love—
you can never explain
to the originals of all these things:
your space,
your time,
your air,
your life,
make the essence of love,"
said Chamundi.

He gave her
music cassettes
and sweetmeats.
Hearing a tinkling laughter,
he said humbly,
"Clamoring
meaningless
obese
words
are all I can offer,
my Little Princess.

Can nothingness
offer plentitude?
Can flesh
offer the cosmos?"

To him who did not
comprehend the act of giving,
Chamundi said:
"Give her
your dreams,
your tears,
your smile,
your silence,
your self."

0°

You are the witch
who has cast me
into nothingness.

You, floating
down a stream as a twig,
are transfiguring me as well.

Now—
"Extreme love will kill you,"
you said, "Do not follow me."
I'm a man who cries torrents
over a dead plant;
you have overwhelmed me.

"Don't you love me?"
I asked.
"No,"
your voice said.
"Can you look into my eyes
and say that?"
With no reply
but a sob
you vanished
into the mirror.

Not knowing how to
liberate you from
the glass,
my ears rent
by your silent screams,
I tried to withdraw
into a long stretch of loneliness
away from the memories of you
I tried to withdraw
into the smell of my solitutde
As I set off,
my nerves shuddered
my veins
exploded
the pain seeped
into the center of my bones.

How can I be separate
from you,
having lost myself
in your black iris?

In the vast universe
floating molecules
collide
somewhere in spacetime.

On a bench
in an deserted train station
you sit alone.
I sit on the next bench
writing a poem.
Our eyes meet;
you show no recognition.

You rise,
walk to the edge of the platform,
and return to sit.
Why are you so tense?
This waiting...
You can't complete the thought.
You don't even know
why you are waiting.

The poem,
the waiting,
the tension
go on.

Turning a poem into reality,
reality into a dream;
is this real?
Or is it real's shadow?
A shadow's dream?
A dream's poem?

0°

Huddled
in my burrow
drowning between
sleep and sleeplessness
Yanni's music
brings me to the surface
A little boy
sits on a porch at noon
A woman's corpse
lies there still kissing her lover
A child's anklet
lies alone
like a crescent
in a starless sky
Eyes stare blankly
out of a shattered face
Somewhere, a dog howls
Dried blood on the path
"Hook
your time
in your poetry,"
mocks the Little Princess's voice

Is it possible to capture
time in a poem?
The living dead
wander the Earth aimlessly.
I stand shocked
staring at
the headless body's
erect penis;
remembering the angry hordes of feminists
out to castrate
poets who dare to valorise love,
I run
and bury myself
beneath the Little Princess's footsteps.
Pretending that
her breath is still lingering
in that dead space,
I begin to search.
From amongst the corpses
crawls out
a weeping child.

0°

Notes from the Sphere of Darkness

On that day
a mute soothsayer
mimed,
You claim
you deny yourself, and your words
but
you
who claim
poetry is dead
will someday
live in
those poems.
He gave no reasons.
Today
if I say
it is my life and blood
that becomes the poem,
you will laugh at me:
"Do not kill me with
your withered words."

What is it then,
that fills my emptiness
and pens the poem?
Is it your silence?
Your writing?
Your eyes
widening in surprise?
Currents flowing from
your enigmatic memory?
Are you really you?
Or are you Chamundi?
Or are you an intangible
mystical symbol?
Don't just dismiss this
as a madman's rambling.
With my poem
I am postponing my death.

0°

Trials

In my previous birth you were my lover
before that you were my mother
and even before that you were my sister.
Before everything, you were
my Chamundi, my God
and before that before that
before that
for ages and ages, I have loved you.
You promised me that in your next birth
you would be my daughter.
I trusted in you
I spoke to the stars
about my daughter-to-be-born,
and to the moon, too.
I imagined that I carried you piggyback
and wandered the forests.
I dreamt that you whispered in my ears,
"Carrying me will strengthen your back."

In the horrific game of nature
even as you were born
you lost your breath and lay dead

I kissed your curled fingers,
slit my body with shards of glass
I bathed you with my streaming blood
I plucked out my single eye
and tucked it into your curled palm
The ancestors' voices screamed at me—
You may have been born dead,
but
before I lower you
back into the Earth's womb
I must give you a name,
they said.
Startled, I wondered:
What do I name you?
I pondered and puzzled
God, as She passed by, said
your name was Genesis

Genny Genny Genny Genny
Genny Genny Genny Genny
Genny
I kissed you from head to toe
and sobbed.
Won't you part those coral lips
and call out my name?
Open those lotus eyes
and look at me?
Extend those delicate feet
and kick me?
Your warm touch
the taste of those lips
grabs my memory
I howl with pain

0°

Expression
that filled the vacuum
of the dead
turned his muscles
to poem
and then froze
into silent rock.

Centuries of pain
were living inside
the rock
as curried fire.

The language of the void
putrefied
and from the rotting eyes
a poem oozed out.

Standing at the edge
of death
with the scorpion clinging to his stomach

223

He plucked out his single eye
and flung it

The rock exploded into
smithereens

The augur, travelling
through the mountains on a train
in the dark, said
"She
was the offering
God loaned to the world."

0°

Shakthi was nothingness
in the void.
Unable to bear
the burden of the emptiness,
to relieve
her pain,
She created
the cosmos and the atom
planets
galaxies
fire
water
air
earth and flowers
forests and deserts
birds and beasts
all these
and many more
Shakthi created.
She roamed the forests, but then,
feeling alone, sat on the seashore

and called down the stars
for company.

The barren desert
was violently desolate.
Neither knowledge nor unknowledge
was of any help—
She created man.

With him
again She roamed
the forests.
By the sea
on the shore
She sat with him
and pointed out the stars

Tiring of the meaningless
company of mortal flesh,
She returned to the forest.
Two serpents
coiled in copulation
entwined in pleasure
The universe trembled

She wondered
was this an apocalyptic storm
a cosmic dance
or a divine drama
Comprehending the barrenness
of the desert
She beckoned the man

Come, have sex with me,
Entwine your body with mine.

Scared,
the man refused
Weary Shakthi
Created a second man
and summoned him,
told him the story of the serpent.
Come, have sex with me,
Entwine your body with mine.

He too refused
petrified with fear

She created
a third man
Even he refused
and ran away

Shakthi withdrew
hating her loneliness

The third man told
the first:
Shakthi,
All-Powerful,
Creator, Protector, Destroyer,
Let's fuck her
Appropriate her powers
Neutralize her!

Thus by treacherous sex
Shakthi's powers were stolen
Creation, Protection, Destruction
The three men divided
the chores amongst themselves
Tired, they returned
to ask Shakthi,
"Where's my chapathi?"

0°

FEBRUARY 4TH

This day is a special day
for it was today
God gifted this world the Little Princess.
The forest-dweller, having nothing to offer
either the known or the unknown,
asked the moon
"Do I have anything
I can give the Little Princess?"
"Don't play with her temper,"
warned the moon.
"Warnings are meant to be
disregarded,"
murmured the forest-dweller.
Here
this day
this moment
this object
is not the abstraction
of any particular.
Awesome and pure
is the dust
touched by your feet.

229

0°

CHAPTER 35

IS THIS REALLY A NOVEL, or merely a bunch of notes thrown together into a book? Nano, Muniyandi, Surya, Misra, Ninth-Century-A.D.-Dead-Brain, Thayumanavan, Genesis, Neena, Shireen, Avanthika, Fuckrunissa, Aarthi, Kottikuppan, Anandhasami, Thirumalai, The Honorable Tamil Writer, Monica, Deepthi, Kavitha… is this just a list of random names? From among the scattered sheaves of paper, the imaginary character Nano asked Muniyandi, *Did you create me just so that posterity would have some record of your existence?* In his memory the past never leaves a trace, and there is no clue about the future. He is constantly at time zero; this zero time is traveling on a line made of uncountably many points, as an imaginary point. You have read all these pages patiently; at this moment, while you are still my reader, I am trekking across the snowy Himalayas. I am leaving you. Since I have emotionally detached myself, leaving you is not sorrowful. What else can I do? Please, go ahead and search for meaning in the host of words scattered in these pages. I try to bring it to a close, but the words keep endlessly pouring out. Our conversation may end here or be followed by an ellipsis or

---

* *The Great Ecstasy of Sculptor Steiner* – film by Werner Herzog
† Renhold Messner in *The Dark Glow of the Mountains* – film by Werner Herzog

There is a ski jump competition in progress. Steiner* has reached a distance of 189 meters. If he had tried for another nine meters, he might have died—or broken the world record.

I had a pet raven. It lost all its feathers. Afterwards, as it was strolling about on the terrace, a murder of crows flew in from somewhere and began to attack it. I tried to chase them away but they would not stop their assault. I ran downstairs, brought up my gun, and shot down my raven. I want to be alone in this world. Humans scare me. Only on these cold slopes do I find solace.

He† is climbing Mount Karakoram in the Himalayas. He loves mountain climbing; he wants to spend the rest of his life doing nothing else but scaling lofty peaks. Once he gets to the summit, he'll search for another mountain and then another and another and another.

The frozen rock towers into the sky. Eighteen thousand feet—it's just a number. The skies and seas and mountains seem to recede from me. Goat **antelope**, which are neither goats nor antelope, are racing around on the icy fields below.

> I've lost count of the days
> Herds of animals, waves of shadow
> A figure leaps into the air
> I am merged with the snowy peak
> Silence
> Wordless empty void
> I want to liberate my thoughts
> from the crashing waves that surround them
> I reject all the words of my life
> to kneel here
> loving you
> Will my very breath now freeze as well?
> Say the Word

Tamil Family Names
and Forms of Address

amma	mother
appa	father
anna	elder brother (or any older man)
akka	elder sister
anni	sister-in-law; elder brother's wife
mama	maternal uncle, or paternal aunt's husband
paati	grandmother, or any old woman
da	informal masculine address
di	feminine address, used with a younger person, or disrespectfully
dey	masculine address, disrespectful or angry

Notes

7 *Existentialism and Fancy Banyan*	the author's first novel, featuring many of the same characters
7 *mayi avaa... thi phutthi*	Hindi: "my sister was dick mom was dick mom was cunt"
9 *randi nondi...kindi kendi*	Some of this is gibberish, some is not: "Streetwalker, cripple, *sondi, pandi, mandi,* ass, pussy crust, milk feeder, *kendi*"
11 "When a banyan tree... the Earth will quake."	Rajiv Gandhi's comment on the anti-Sikh riots of 1984 following Indira Gandhi's assassination
11 *Aatha Un Koyilile*	*Mother, in Your Temple*—a 1991 Tamil film

11	*En Pottukku Sondhakaaran*	*The Owner of my Pottu* (bindi)—not an actual film
11	*En Purushan Thaan Enakku Mattum Thaan*	*My Husband is Mine Alone*—a 1989 Tamil film
12	Patwari	member of a landowning caste
12	poromboke	land that is neither owned by any individual nor specifically state-owned
18	lathi	policeman's baton
22	*Puratchithilakam*	*Jewel of the Revolution*—not an actual film
22	*Puratchithilakam I.P.S.*	*Jewel of the Revolution, Indian Police Service*
22	*ahimsa*	policy of non-violence as advocated by Mahatma Gandhi
22	*Radhika... Rajyasri, RAW*	these are names of film actresses, all starting with the Tamil letter *ra*; RAW is also the acronym of the Research and Analysis Wing, India's external intelligence agency
22	*Pullukul Kal*	*Stone Inside a Blade of Grass*—not an actual film
23	Jayasudha... Banupriya	well-known film actresses
26	zarda beeda	betel leaf packed with strong tobacco
27	Santhal tribe	the largest tribal community in India; 10,000 Santhals rebelled against the British colonists in 1855
29	maravan	member of the Mukkulathor caste
31	Margazhi	ninth month of the Tamil calendar; December 15-January 14
31	Kurumbur Kuppusami	writer of Tamil pulp fiction active in the mid-20th century
32	Parveen Babi	Hindi film actress popular in the 1970s

34	*Maa aapsanket...* *jhoothe banaata houn*	Hindi: "Because my Mom is having sex, I have to lie around in your room"
34	*Arrey bachche, teri maa kithar gayee?*	Hindi: "Hey kid, where's your mother gone?"
35	punkawallah	manual fan operator
36	ghazal	a poetic musical form from North India
40	didi	elder sister or cousin—in this case, the elder brother's wife (Hindi)
41	beti	daughter, in this case daughter-in-law (Hindi)
42	gopuram	tapering South Indian temple tower
44	pallangkuzhi	a game played with cowry shells; a form of mancala
44	thumri	a Hindustani semi-classical music composition
47	Aryan yoni	"Aryan", here as in all of India, is understood to indicate descent from those who came from Central Asia over the Khyber Pass in prehistory, especially members of the Brahmin and Kshatriya castes—as opposed to ethnic Dravidians. Yoni, of course, is Sanskrit for vagina
48	Karuppan	a Tamil man's name meaning "black"
58	*Kannathil muthumittal...*	lyrics by Bharathiyar, early 20th century Tamil poet
60	vaal	Tamil for the sound of a dog's bark
63	a minister in your country... to eat rats	this is a reference to comments made by Lalu Prasad Yadav, former Chief Minister of the state of Bihar
67	defile	the word here is *karpazhippu*, literally "to erase a woman's chastity", formerly used as a euphemism for sexual abuse/rape in the Tamil media. In 1986, the National Women's Front agitated successfully to end the use of this word (and its analogs in other Indian languages) because of the implication that

235

		sex with an "unchaste" woman is never rape. It was replaced in Tamil with *balatkaaram*, "to sexually overpower"
68	Mudevi	goddess of bad luck; opposite of Sridevi
69	pallu	the end of a sari that is left free to cover the woman's chest
69	*phir bhi*	Hindi: "in spite of that"
69	sign	the word used is *kuri*, which signifies both "sign" and "penis"
72	*vilambit*	an introductory slow tempo in Hindustani classical music
75	dhaba	roadside cafeteria
76	Lal Salaam	Hindi: "Red Salute." Typically used by communists throughout South Asia both as a greeting and a goodbye
78 Thayumanavan… and this is how they named me		Thayumanavan is a Hindu name, meaning "he who is also the mother." The historical figure Thayumanavar (eighteenth century?) composed mystical poems in Tamil combining the philosophies of Vedanta and Saiva Siddhanta
81	Bheeman	second Pandava brother in the *Mahabharatam*
81	Duryodhanan	eldest Kaurava brother in the *Mahabharatam*
86	veshti	a four-yard length of cloth worn on the lower body by men
87	varma	martial art practiced in Kerala
87	bharatanatyam	classical dance of South India
87	sacred thread	*poonal*, a white thread worn around the shoulder by men of the "upper" castes (Brahmins, etc.), signifying that they have been "twice-born"
87	chappals	sandals, slippers
92	Pichamurthi	Naa. Pichamurthi, a well-known 20th century Tamil writer

97 *Kokogam*	any of several ancient Tamil manuscripts on sex
97 A woman named Kannagi… I am Ilango	Ilango Adigal was the author of the 5th century Tamil epic Silappathikaaram, of which Kannagi is the heroine. Kannagi tears off her breast and throws it on town of Madurai, thereby burning it down. This is contrasted with the 1997 bombing of the Pandian Express train to Madurai
114 Hanle	site of the Indian Astronomical Observatory
114 Nano mi vida, Nano mi niña	Spanish: "Nano my life, Nano my baby girl"
121 algunos aspectos del cuento	Spanish: "some aspects of the count"
122 suburbs	the understanding here is of lower-middle-class neighborhoods surrounding the (wealthier) city
123 Nine fruits for nine rupees	the word used is actually *ombodhu*, which means eunuch (hijra), instead of *onpadhu*, nine
129 Brihanalai	in the *Mahabharatam*, the disguise Arjunan assumes in the thirteenth year of his exile, as the eunuch dance teacher of Princess Uthara
130 record dance	a dance show given on a small platform on a street corner by a woman or eunuch dressed in heavily-sequined bra and panties, dancing to raunchy film songs, typically with a man riding a bicycle around and around the gathered crowd for hours into the night
133 my younger sister's daughter	while marriage to a cross cousin (father's sister's son or mother's brother's son) would be considered favorable, Aarthi's marriage to a parallel cousin is considered incestuous
134 thevidiya	literally woman wedded to God; traditionally, a member of a caste of temple-dancers, used sexually by the feudal lords and temple trustees. The practice was officially abolished in 1934; the term survives as an insult

138 arivaalmanai	blade fixed to a piece of wood, used for chopping vegetables
142 naina	father (Telugu)
154 Azhagi	beauty, beautiful one
158 panchayat	district-level elected body
163 thali and a pair of toe-rings	both are symbols of a married South Indian Hindu woman. The thali is a gold chain or turmeric-smeared cord, tied around the woman's neck by the groom in the wedding ceremony
163 Amman	goddess
166 Seth	North Indian pawnbroker
173 St. Thomas Mount	the Tamil name Parangimalai, literally "white man's hill," is used
174 Copper T	a type of intrauterine contraceptive device
174 slokas	Sanskrit prayers
181 annas	1/16th of a rupee, an obsolete denomination
183 *Prabanja Kaalam*	*The Universal Times*; not an actual newspaper
184 ...Brahminized the entire Gounder culture	the majority of the Gounder caste supported the atheist-leaning, anti-Brahmin Dravidian Movement of the 1950s, known for non-religious "self-respect" weddings
185 vallaikappu	ceremony held in the seventh month of a woman's first pregnancy
191 *"Vills hai?" "Vills nahi hai"*	Hindi: "Do you have Wills [cigarettes]?" "No, no Wills."
192 matkas	small handmade clay cups, used and then discarded
192 Nappinnai	another name for Aandal, the poet, referring to herself in the third person as Krishna's lover
192 Madhava	a name of Krishna
192 Kannan	a name of Krishna

192	harikatha	a form of devotional storytelling
193	Perumal… Ranga	Ranganathan Perumal is an avatar of Vishnu. This is *nindhastudi*, a way of talking to God where the petitioner demands blessings, without formal respect
197	Yakshan	a mythical creature; something like a sphinx, but able to take different forms
198	*bechara*	Hindi: "poor child", "urchin"
199	*Delhi to dilwale ka hai!*	Hindi: "Delhi is for the brave at heart!"
199	Vikramadithyan's vampire	the monster from the story *Vetala Panchvimshati*, who searches for a soul to sacrifice for its own redemption
201	Sukran	the god of the planet Venus, who is obsessed with love for his daughter
202	Karnan	a character in the *Mahabharatam* known for his extreme generosity
202	Thilothama	one of the four apsaras (celestial nymphs) in Lord Indra's court

ABOUT THE AUTHOR

Charu Nivedita grew up in rural Tamil Nadu and spent twelve years working in Delhi before moving to Chennai. He has written three novels, one short story collection and several political commentaries, and for the past five years has been writing regular columns which are translated into Malayalam for the journals *Madhyamam* (on contemporary Arabic literature), *Kala Kaumudhi* (on politics), and *Mathru Bhoomi* (on world music). His latest "mega novel" *Raasa Leela* has been serialized in *Kala Kaumudhi*.

ABOUT THE TRANSLATORS

Pritham K. Chakravarthy is a theatre artist, storyteller, activist, freelance scholar, and translator based in Chennai. Her recent translation projects include *The Blaft Anthology of Tamil Pulp Fiction*, also available from Blaft Publications.

Rakesh Khanna was born in Berkeley, California. He has lived in Chennai since 1998 working as an editor for an e-learning website.